# SPARE PARTS

# SPARE PARTS

## MARSHALL HIGHET

ARCHWAY
PUBLISHING

Archway Publishing books may be ordered through booksellers or by contacting:

Archway Publishing
1663 Liberty Drive
Bloomington, IN 47403
www.archwaypublishing.com
1-(888)-242-5904

Because of the dynamic nature of the Internet, any web addresses or
links contained in this book may have changed since publication and
may no longer be valid. The views expressed in this work are solely those
of the author and do not necessarily reflect the views of the publisher,
and the publisher hereby disclaims any responsibility for them.

Any people depicted in stock imagery provided by Thinkstock are models,
and such images are being used for illustrative purposes only.
Certain stock imagery © Thinkstock.

ISBN: 978-1-4808-0862-1 (sc)
ISBN: 978-1-4808-0864-5 (hc)
ISBN: 978-1-4808-0863-8 (e)

Library of Congress Control Number: 2014914275

Printed in the United States of America.

Archway Publishing rev. date: 10/17/2014

For Kian and Bryan Lea

From a wild weird clime that lieth, sublime,
Out of Space—out of Time.
Edgar Allan Poe *Dreamland*

.

# CHAPTER ONE

Lynx, Slug and LeftEye were working the crowd at the bazaar. Lynx looked up from his post, feeling the falling drops dappling his face. He smiled. It was Raintime in Middlespace, exactly three o'clock. They were counting on this uniform downpour, which drenched the plants growing from every rooftop and open area, to help disguise their actions.

Today, Lynx would be Scout for the team of teenagers. It was Slug's turn to be Point and LeftEye was, grudgingly, Distract. As Lynx watched the bustling marketplace for easy marks, Slug and LeftEye remained an equidistance apart. The plaza was packed with vendors hawking their goods, mostly Middlespacers with an occasional A-One strolling by. The boys moved in a loose phalanx, keeping one another in view, as they drifted through the miasma of bodies and carts like jellyfish floating through a seaweed forest on an underwater current.

Lynx was out front, scanning the people around him for vulnerabilities. Ahead of him, an older woman in a saffron-colored robe, muddied at the hem, was haggling with a vendor about a wreath of tiny hot peppers she was waving in the air. Their bright greens and reds made a stark contrast to her robe. Her toothless mouth flapped as she grew more agitated. She dropped her leather bag at her feet in her enthusiasm as she countered the vendor's obviously high price. Lynx turned his head imperceptibly to the right, toward LeftEye, and jerked his chin toward the old woman. He then stationed himself next to a wall to watch the action, his job momentarily done.

LeftEye whipped a harmonica out from the sleeve of his soiled coat and honked on it abruptly. A circle of people, along with the vendor and old woman, turned to watch. He took a breath, pulled back his hood to expose his face—glowing laser eye included—and began playing a tune with a hectic beat, tapping his foot in unison. The small crowd stood entranced for a moment as his music took hold. Slug crouched next to the vendor's stall and snaked a hand into the woman's purse, lying by her feet. He rummaged through it, eventually drawing out an electronic wallet. This he tucked into his waistband as he backed slowly away from the stall, still in a crouch. Seeing Slug's retreat, Lynx gave LeftEye another nod. The song came to an intense crescendo and he finished with a flourish. The crowd erupted into applause, and the oblivious old woman turned back to her beef with the vendor, still shaking the wreath of peppers. The boys melted into the crowd and collected themselves behind a bookseller.

"What's she got?" LeftEye said as Slug scrolled through the wallet's contents.

"Not enough. We'll have to hit some more marks to make it worthwhile," Slug responded.

"Do you guys ever feel bad about this?" Lynx asked abruptly, causing both his friends to stare at him.

"About what?" Slug asked, his fingertip poised on the touchpad.

"You know, stealing." Lynx's olive skin turned red with the intensity of his friends' glares.

"No! Why should we? I mean, Botches have no other way of getting currency." LeftEye was defensive. "With no means to earn a proper wage, we have to make our own opportunities, yeah?" He looked to Slug for agreement.

"That's right, I mean, how are we supposed to feed the family? How would that do for Wren and Phlox?" Slug asked pointedly, bringing it home for Lynx.

"I know, I know, it's just ... sometimes it feels *wrong*." Lynx held his hands out in appeasement.

"We gotta do what we gotta do." Slug tucked the wallet back into his waistband. His eyebrows came down in a severe line as he studied Lynx. "Are you still in or do we need to find another Scout?"

"No, no, I'm still in." Lynx looked at the rain making puddles in between the cobblestones. "Forget I said anything."

The next mark Lynx spotted was a couple in their forties. Their clothes identified them as Middlespacers: sturdy, functional, and worn at the seams, but not quite as worn as Botches' clothes and not quite as fine as A-Ones'. Lynx was about to signal LeftEye to start up the band again when a tall form with a gossamer headpiece covering her face moved through the rain behind the couple and turned a corner. Lynx stopped, his eyes following the seemingly crystalline creature until she disappeared.

*What the ...* Lynx picked up his pace to follow her, not checking to see if the others were behind him or not. As he turned the corner, he glimpsed her pale gown moving through the swarm of bodies. He craned his head but the crowd bottlenecked through a small passage and he lost sight of her. Lynx stopped as LeftEye and Slug came up behind him.

"Anyone?" Slug asked, scanning the crowd.

"Did you see her?" Lynx asked, hand shading his eyes from the rain as he searched for her figure.

"See who? The next mark?"

"An A-One, a girl? Pale dress, this veil thing covering her face. Did you?"

Slug and LeftEye looked at one another skeptically and then back to Lynx.

"A vulture?" LeftEye asked. "Dude, are you feeling okay today?"

Lynx gave up his search for the girl, although the image of her was burned onto his retinas. "Yeah, yeah. Sorry. Vultures our age aren't in Middlespace a lot. Took me by surprise." He put on his game face and watched the ebb and flow of people in front of him. "Hey," he said, his mind back on his task. "Is that another A-One right there? The one in the cloak?"

A tall man was dressed in a fashionably short gray cloak, which the boys were fans of because it was easier to pickpocket.

"And you know what, fellas?" Lynx added, "I bet his electronic wallet is full, maybe even with currbytes."

Slug sidled up as the man stopped to examine some dried crickets that were as large as loaves of bread and ready for boiling. As the man was leaning down, Slug slipped his hand underneath the thick fabric of the cloak, hunting for the satchel that most men wore against their backs. But the man whirled and grabbed Slug's wrist, the hood of the stranger's cloak falling back to reveal his tightened jaw and red curly hair.

"Not today, scavenger," the man growled. "Actually, I'm glad you did that. It gives me an excuse to do *this*."

Slug's eyes went glassy with surprise as the man reached under his cloak, pulled out a black tube, and pressed a button. It began to glow, filling the air with the crackle and acrid scent of a lasertube, which he aimed at Slug's chest. Suddenly, a fiery blast sliced between Slug and the man, sizzling the man's arm and leaving a black tear in the heavy fabric of his cloak. Ten feet away, LeftEye raised his hood, covering the glowing red eye that had shot the laser.

"What the?!?!?" the man screamed, jerking his arm back. Released from the stranger's iron grip, Slug was off, ducking and dodging through the throng of shoppers and hawkers. The man barrelled after him, bellowing as he went. Lynx sprinted after them at a distance, sure that LeftEye was close behind. Slug ran for all he was worth, but the gray-cloaked man was closing the gap. When Slug glanced back to gauge the distance between them, the man's fingers brushed the back of Slug's coat, caught, and grabbed again, finding fabric and jerking Slug backwards. Slug fumbled with the clasp at his throat, releasing his jacket.

*Man, his mother is going to kill him for losing that,* Lynx thought as the man threw Slug's coat to the ground and picked up speed.

But Slug, now freed of the constricting coat, took a small hop on his tricked-out metal legs and leapt over a mini-vegetable hovercart. The man in the gray cloak blasted the cart with his lasertube, spraying tiny tomatoes and small squash everywhere as the vendor jumped out of the way. Lynx followed, feet sliding on the liquefied remnants of the vegetables.

Slug was at his maximum, the pistons in his long silver legs working feverishly as he ricocheted against walls and bounded over hovercarts and transports. The rain was tapering off; it occurred to Lynx that it must be close to 3:30. Slug reached the second wall, the one separating Middlespace from the edge of the Dome. Fear gripped Lynx. There was nowhere to go out there. The Dome reached up in a never ending arc, its surface pitted by storms whipping gritty sand against it.

Slug was halfway up the wall, the metal claws protruding from his rectangular feet scrabbling for footholds on the rain-slick wall. His hand reached the top and Lynx thought he'd made it, but the man leapt up, catching Slug around his metal ankle and dragging him to the cobblestones below in an inglorious thump.

"Now I have you, freak. You think you can get away with stealing from an Evolutionist?" the man screamed, his reddish curls dripping rain and sweat onto Slug's face. He raised his hand, fist curled around the glowing tube. Without thinking, Lynx unhinged his left hand from the rest of his metal arm and leveled a blast at the man. A sizzling beam shot out of Lynx's wrist, the heat kicking back onto his face. The man screamed. All that was left of his fist was a seared and cauterized stump.

Slug turned a shocked gaze on Lynx, shaking his head in awe, and jumped over the fallen A-One to bound down an alley. Left Eye, hood hiding half of his face, beckoned Lynx to follow them as he melted into the darkness after Slug. Lynx, shaken, started after them, but a man in similar gray blocked his way, grabbing his arm and dragging him back.

"You. Are. Dead." The red-haired A-One was bent over, spit dripping from his lips as he rose with effort. The reddish freckles that spangled across his nose stood out against his pallid skin. The rain had stopped right on schedule and the streets steamed, giving the crowded corner the air of a jungle. The A-One stumbled, and then straightened, wincing as he tucked his wounded hand into his shirt.

"Give me your tube!" He yelled at the other man.

"Darwin," the man replied. "Do you really think that's a good i ..."

"Tube!" Darwin hollered.

The man slapped a tube into Darwin's outstretched hand.

"You're going to pay for this! This will show you the price of loyalty. You Underdwellers don't have friends," Darwin's voice rose, causing people to stare. "Underdwellers don't have family. Get him to his knees." The other man forced Lynx down to the glossy cobblestones. Leveling the lasertube at Lynx's face, Darwin leaned down and growled, "You aren't allowed to love."

Lynx willed himself to keep his eyes open wide, to watch his murderer make the last move. Darwin grimaced, half snarl and half smile, and energized the tube to a lethal glowing yellow.

"You will NOT!" A voice ricocheted across the courtyard, silencing the curious murmurs of the crowd. Darwin whipped his head in the direction of the voice, his grimace turning to an "O" of disbelief at the sight of the veiled A-One who had distracted Lynx earlier. When she reached the two A-Ones and Lynx, her gloved hands pulled back her veil to reveal an oval face, delicately arched dark brows, and hair like a waterfall in winter. She glanced at Lynx with curiosity, and then returned her translucent gaze to Darwin.

"You *will* spare him." The figure clasped her hands and stepped in between Lynx and Darwin, causing the enraged man to stumble backwards on the uneven cobblestones.

"But, he … my hand. Did you see what he did? You can't!" Darwin sputtered.

"I can, and I will," she commanded. Lynx fixed his attention on the hem of her dress hovering above the ground. "You will install a new hand by this evening, I am sure."

"That's not the point!" He roared in her face. "An Underdweller blasted my hand off!" He shook the severed stump in her face for punctuation. Around him, the crowd cringed. The girl didn't move. Mist swirled around her floating dress like a pet cat.

"Leave him to me. If you are unsure about my authority in a case such as this, I suggest you check with your programmer."

"You bet I will," Darwin spat. "And your production code is?"

"I am X3721, product of QN210 and KG727."

Darwin blanched, his good arm dropping to his side like a coin through water. He stood his ground for another moment, his facial features working. Finally he spun around, his cloak spinning with him. "Come on," he coughed to his friend. As he strode by the girl in silver, he leaned in close, hissing, "I hope to Dome you know what you're doing." Pausing next to Lynx, he spat onto the cobblestones in front of the boy's kneeling form. "You lucked out today, but don't imagine for a moment that I'll forget that pretty face of yours. Remember what I said: Underdwellers don't have feelings." Then he was gone into the eddying mist. His henchman followed, but only after giving the statuesque girl one more wondering glance.

Lynx rose, taking a moment to readjust his metal hand securely on his wrist and covering it with his sleeve. When he raised his gaze, the silver girl had turned to him. She came to just his shoulder but her bearing made her seem taller. She was still, hands clasped in front of her, brows arched, seeming as if she hadn't moved at all. But her eyes glinted with something that Lynx wasn't accustomed to seeing on an A-One's face. Was that a smile? Yes, it seemed as if her lilac-tinted lips folded almost imperceptibly at the corners.

"Thank you," Lynx said, ducking his head as all Underdwellers must in the presence of an A-One. He stared at the hovering hem of her dress, awaiting an order or a condemnation from her. After many moments of silence, he looked at her quizzically.

"That was ... very unusual." Her voice had lost its imperious quality. She sounded amused and slightly awed. "Walk with me," she commanded, pulling the veil over her face and floating through the crowd, parting it like the mist.

# CHAPTER TWO

ynx followed, still shaking. After a few turns through the warren of noisy, narrow streets crowded with hovercarts, buyers and sellers, and an assortment of smells thick enough to suffocate, the silvery A-One turned down an alley. The scent of flowers and growing plants wafted toward them and the green of a garden in sunlight glinted from half a block down. They came to a private place that Lynx had never seen before. Vines climbed around columns, weaving together overhead and blocking out Middlespace and, above that, the ivory towers and floating discs that were home to the A-Ones. Mauve blossoms hung down like bunched grapes, their scent masking the blended city smell that permeated the air in Middlespace.

Lynx explored the garden in wonder. In the center of the flagstone circle was a fountain with a stone-scaled fish spurting water into an onyx pool. Replicas of other fish swam in halting circles. Lynx let out a low whistle of appreciation and turned back to the girl. She sat on a bench next to the fountain, face unveiled, hands still clasped. She cocked her head as she observed him, the almost-undetectable smile once again hovering around her mouth.

He stepped toward her and, with a sudden impulse, bowed. Her laughter sounded like icicles breaking one after another. "Oh my," she said to the crown of his head. "You must be from another time, a time of knights and ladies."

He rose, swiping at the swath of dark hair falling in his eyes. "Thank you, again. You saved me. If it weren't for you …"

She waved her hand. "Stop. It's you who saved yourself."

"What do you mean?"

She paused, watching petals drift down to dimple the dark surface of the water. "Isn't it beautiful here? My producers, I mean my parents, built it."

"Why would they do that?" Lynx asked. "A-Ones generally stay Above, so why make this where they couldn't enjoy it?"

"They thought it would raise morale for the Middlespacers. They think more outside the box than other A-Ones," she said, bowing her head a fraction.

"I guess so." Lynx took in the white marble columns and the fancy fountain, calculating the hours and expense needed to create such a place. And for no other reason than enjoyment, not even their own enjoyment it seemed. *Different types of A-Ones indeed.*

"I can tell that you're not like the others," Lynx said to the girl.

"Yes, I am, I'm exactly like the rest of them: perfect in my construction."

"You laughed. A-Ones don't laugh, especially not with Botches."

The curious glint came back to her eyes. "Of course we laugh! And why do you call yourselves Botches? How interesting." It was impossible to tell what color her eyes were. They were almost colorless with a hint of gray green, her irises blending with the whites of her eyes with only the slightest change in pigment. He imagined they must be the same color as the moon—the few times he'd seen the moon. He realized he was staring at her, and she returned his gaze, giving him courage.

"What do you mean about saving myself?"

"I meant when you saved your friend. You sacrificed yourself to save him. I find that rare. Quite a show of loyalty. I've been taught that Underdwellers, 'Botches' I mean, do not have the faculties of loyalty or bravery."

"And I was taught that A-Ones don't laugh. So we're obviously both wrong," Lynx said defensively.

"Obviously," she leveled back at him. "Pride too." She leaned toward him; Lynx's heart stalled for a few moments and then began again at triple speed.

"So," he began again. "You saved me because I saved Slug."

Her tinkling laughter filled the green space. "Slug," she said. "What a funny name." Lynx liked her laugh and planned on hearing it as much as possible.

"We call him that because when he takes off his legs he looks like a slug without them. It's a little mean but he's my brother. It's also funny because, you know, when he's wearing them, he's not sluggish at all."

"Family units too. Interesting."

"Well, my adopted brother really ..."

"And you? What do they call you?"

"Me? I'm Lynx," he grinned, a bright white crescent in his olive-skinned face.

"Lynx." The way she teased the word out on her tongue made his cheeks itch.

"And what about you? Are you always called X3721?"

"No, that's my identifying number, to let others know my level and who my producers are. You may call me Tesla."

"Tesla." He repeated. "Tesla, how can I repay you? You may think that I saved myself, but without you, I'd be a puddle of atoms on the street, waiting for some robosweeper to suck up my remains. I owe you. And where I come from, we always pay our debts. No matter what."

Tesla looked at her hands for a moment. "There is one thing."

"Anything."

"Anything, you say?" She looked at him fully and it was like a physical blow to be this close to her see-through eyes. "I want to go down there. I want to go Below."

For a moment, Lynx couldn't speak. His tongue was a stone in his mouth. The words echoed in his head, vibrating against his skull.

"Go Below?" Lynx said when he could speak. "But that's impossible!"

She watched him from the bench. Her dress floated serenely around her legs. "I want you to take me there." The mischievous glint appeared in her eyes. "You did say you'd do *anything* to repay me."

Lynx sputtered, digging for a reason to say no. After a few moments, he shook his head in defeat. "We'll need to find you a disguise," he said, not meeting her gaze. "You'll stick out like an A-One down there in that get-up."

"Oh, it won't be today," Tesla amended, standing and scattering the pool of petals that had gathered in the folds of her gossamer dress. She placed an oval object the size of a pocket watch in Lynx's hand. "We'll go tomorrow. When this begins to glow, meet me here in one hour." She covered the object lying in Lynx's palm with her own. Lynx was startled by the coldness of her skin. Seeing his reaction, Tesla pulled her hand back, stuffing it in the side of her dress.

"It will glow *and* vibrate when I've activated it. Remember," she said as she backed away through the vines. "One hour. Be here. Repay your debt."

Beyond the row of columns, she punched numbers into the clear communicator on her wrist and held it in the air. Her sleeve slipped down the alabaster length of her arm as a shaft of blue light enveloped her from above. When the levitation beam pulled her into the air, floating her diamond bright hair around her like a nimbus, she grinned at Lynx. He returned the smile, smitten by its boldness. Then she was gone, leaving him alone in the garden, oval stone in hand.

Lynx fumbled with the leather satchel at his waist, tucking the opaque stone into it and pulling the drawstring tight. *Oh Dome, what have I done?* Lynx wondered as he looked around, heading out of the small garden and into the alley. *An A-One Below? What's gotten into me?* Then Tesla's face drifted through his mind: first the icy demeanor she'd presented to the Evolutionists, and then her delighted visage when he'd agreed to take her Below.

*I've never seen anyone so excited,* Lynx thought as he made a series of quick turns. He knew the route so well that he didn't have to think about his path through the marketplace. The vendors were packing up their hovercarts, readying to go home in Middlespace. Lynx jogged over the cobblestones. The air still smelled of humans pressed together mixed with a smattering of spices and sweat.

Lynx took a left at the end of the emptying street. Halfway down the alley, he stopped at the side entrance of a vacant building. An opening stretched up for twelve feet where a window used to be, possibly repossessed to be used in an A-One residence Above. Lynx glanced up at the darkening sky to the pearl-colored tower over him, branches unfurling toward the edges of the Dome. A few of the globes and discs that hung off them like polyps were coming to life in soft colors of peach and blue as the A-Ones returned home from whatever wholesome activity had kept them occupied for the afternoon.

Lynx stepped through the empty window casing and walked toward the banks of dark elevators, choosing the second to last one on the right; he twisted a metal wheel embedded at the top of its door. It cranked open and Lynx stood at the edge, waiting for his eyes to adjust to the gloom before leaping into the darkness.

He landed on the top of the car and yanked at a wire hanging to the left of the doors, clanging them shut. He opened the electrical compartment and fired up the laser in his metallic pointer finger. His face was illuminated as he worked, disconnecting three key wires and reconnecting them at certain ports. As he soldered the second wire, the car shuddered, and at the third one, it jumped in the close shaft, electricity humming through it.

From below him an automated female voice said, "What floor please? Currently, you are in the sub main floor. Up or down please?" Lynx leaned his face close to the panel, his jaw and cheekbones lit up by the glowing buttons. "Sub 33,' he said, enunciating each syllable.

"Sub 33," the voice agreed. "Arrival in forty-six seconds."

Lynx wrapped his metal fingers around the cable attached to the top of the elevator as the car began gliding downward. The lit outline of the closed doors above him lifted away into the darkness. It was the last of Middlespace he would see until Tesla summoned him.

# CHAPTER THREE

esla's hair lifted around her shoulders as the transport beam pulled her through the air. She was quickly drawn away from the steaming streets of Middlespace, with its crowded market and throngs of smelly people. She rotated in the beam as she ascended, craning her neck to keep the green garden in view. The white tower of the A-Ones narrowed the higher she got, finally spreading to create a web above her, with circular domiciles hanging in groups from every branch. The transporter beam shifted its course to weave through the bone-colored neighborhoods. As she sailed past each group of living spaces, the lights came on as A-Ones returned home. At the very top of the tree-like structure, Tesla reached an oval platform, her silver-tipped shoes touching down as the transporter beam dissipated in a shower of sparks. Her wrist communicator went dark. As she strode across the platform toward an entryway, she glanced across the chasm of space between the landing pad and her home and saw her mother moving around in the kitchen behind tinted glass. At the doorway, the circular doors swung inward, admitting her to the metal and ivory foyer.

Pulling away her headpiece and unfastening her cloak, she hung them on a hook near the door, which automatically moved toward a closet at the far end. A small yip echoed from the adjoining room and a fluffy white dog came bounding into the entrance hall.

"Hello Pav, love." Tesla knelt down to pet the pup, who skidded to a halt and looked up at her, tongue lolling. The image of him shimmered as Tesla reached out a hand to stroke his back, her fingers passing through his fur as he blurred.

She straightened and walked through the oval doorway into a living room done in whites and grays. She skipped down three steps, passing a translucent piano, whose keys lit up as the sensors detected her movement.

"Not now," she commanded the piano, which darkened. She leapt up the three steps to the kitchen.

Her mother stood at a stainless steel counter, typing directives into the glowing face of the stove while Carver, their holographic chef, perched on the edge of the counter. At the bank of refrigerators, Tesla read the screens which listed the contents of each.

"Kinsey," Tesla said, pushing one entry. "We're totally out of kombucha, and Pav's got a serious glitch."

Responding to his name, the small dog yipped at Tesla's feet as she retrieved a bottle of green juice. She looked down as his outline blurred once again. "See?"

"Well, go tell the mech maid about it," Kinsey said distractedly, pushing her cloud of white hair off her forehead with the back of her hand. "Carver and I are up to our eyeballs with this recipe."

"Eyeballs?" The twelve-inch holograph stood and strode over to the touchpad. He peered down into the glowing blue rectangle. "I don't see any eyeballs listed in this one, Ma'am."

"Oh, can it, Carver." Kinsey snapped, swiping a hand through the small image of a person complete with a chef's toque.

"A can of what?" Carver asked, unperturbed by the large hand waving through his body. "Again, Ma'am, I don't see the recipe calling for a can of anything. Although you know what would really work? Peanuts."

Kinsey stabbed at a few buttons on her touchpad and Carver

blinked off and on once, then disappeared altogether. "Always with the peanuts," she muttered. She looked up at her daughter, dark brows arching over similarly pale eyes. "Hello dear, how was your day?"

Tesla drifted over to one of the stools and sat down across from her mother, readjusting the high collar of her dress. "Oh, you know," she commented vaguely as she unscrewed the top of the bottle and took a sip. "Yours?"

"You can guess how mine went from my little exchange with Carver. I swear all of them are considering mutiny today. The mech maid was gone, just gone, for two hours this afternoon! And the dinner we're throwing for your father's imminent promotion is tonight. I considered flipping the switch on the whole lot of them."

"Probably not the best idea," Tesla drawled. "Especially with that dinner tonight."

"Agreed." Kinsey fixed her daughter with her coin-bright eyes. "I'd like you to make an appearance tonight, Tes. We produced a new outfit for you specially."

Tesla groaned, "C'mon, primary producer, do I really have to?"

"Yes, you do, secondary output," Kinsey admonished, reaching to the side of the sink where a small green garden filled with herbs and tiny vegetables grew, and picked a handful of marble-sized tomatoes off a vine. "Now shoo and let me sort this out."

Tesla groaned again and stood to leave, with Pav beside her. "Oh and Kinsey," she said, slipping her hand in her pocket to cup the oval stone there. "I'm going to Avicenna's module tomorrow. We're going to work on that final project and she asked me to spend the night."

"That sounds acceptable," Kinsey was scrolling her touchpad. "When I don't want him around, he's in my face. And then when I need him, poof, he's gone." She leaned close to the glowing blue screen. "Carver! Where in Dome are you?"

Tesla chuckled, rolling her eyes at Pav. "I don't think that's the way it works."

"Don't talk back to your elders, product number two," Kinsey quipped as Tesla left the room. "I programmed you, and I can deprogram you if I want to."

Tesla trotted down the long hallway with Pav close at her heels. Cocoon-shaped lights glowed at her passing and dimmed in her wake. When she reached her room, the sensor scanned her body and the translucent door slid open. She'd tried to reprogram the scanner so that she would be the only one who could enter the room, but her father, Skinner, had overridden her code in about a minute.

*That's what happens when your dad's an expert programmer. No fun at all.* She placed her drink on the plexiglass desk and threw herself onto the circular bed. Her room was furnished in light blues and grays because these neutral hues were more soothing to the A-One's sophisticated sensibilities, as her mother often opined.

She noticed a garment bag next to her on the coverlet. Unwrapping a light gray dress, she held the gown up to her body and sighed. It was gorgeous, of course. Her mother had impeccable taste. The hem and seams were outlined with tiny embedded lights, running up over the hips, under the bodice, and down the arms. A gossamer scarf floated around the shoulders. She just wished that her mother could trust her to pick out her own gown, just once. It hadn't happened yet, but maybe the year she turned eighteen.

*So long to go!* Tesla thought as she flung the gown on a moss green chaise at the entrance of her bathroom. *Three years is way too long for this "curtsey, yes ma'am, yes sir" stuff.*

She stalked into the pale pink bathroom and ran her palm over a raised section of the wall. The lights surrounding the oval mirror blinked once and then dimmed.

"Rainforest, dawn," Tesla said as she turned to a bank of nozzles and faucets. The walls shimmered and then faded to black except for the lights around the mirror. The trills, clacks, and keens of birds became louder as the room brightened, revealing walls that were now a sea of rustling green with the sunlight just peeping through.

Tesla waved her hand in front of a raised rectangle next to the shower, "All four, velocity 3, heat 10." Water spurted from the four jets. She tapped the screen twice, saying "Pink," and the water frothed pink. "Steam," Tesla said as she stripped and stepped into the tiled chamber, leaning back into its billowing warmth.

Newly cleansed, in her bathrobe, and anointed with the various potions and tonics from her medicine cabinet, Tesla stood over the dress laying on her chaise, tapping her foot impatiently. She called out, "Mirror!" and one of the walls shimmered, turning reflective. She stood in front of it and, in a commanding voice, said "Black leather pants, studded tee, spiked collar."

Her reflection blurred until a black-garbed Tesla regarded her real self. Tesla nodded. "Red lipstick, black eyeliner." Instantly the changes were made. *Now that's more like it.*

Quick steps down the hallway startled her. She waved a hand in front of the control board, erasing the goth Tesla and replacing her with a squeaky-clean bathrobed fifteen year old.

Tesla stood before her bed, staring into the smoky opaqueness of her door. A figure appeared behind it as the door slid upward. Lilly bounded in, followed by the quick shadow of her cat.

"Hiya Sis," Lilly said as she dropped into a chair, spinning it with her oversized pink fur boots.

"Lilly. Cat," Tesla greeted them in her most imperious voice. Pav, on the bed, growled himself into a fit of glitches, every escalating yip accompanied with a spasmodic tremor in his body. "Geez, Lilly, can't you keep it out of here? See what it's doing to Pav?" Tesla walked over to the bed and picked up the frothing dog. "Sshhhhh, Pav, calm down. It's Lilly's cat, and you know it'll ..."

At that moment, the black cat looked up, blinked, and seemed to disappear, only to reappear on Lilly's lap, which sent the dog into extreme convulsions, yipping and barking up a storm. Tesla swore that the cat smiled at her.

"That is so flipping creepy, Lill." Tesla's nose creased in distaste. "Why does Schrofinger *do* that?"

"It's SchroDINGer, Tes. And I don't think it's creepy. I think it's epic awesomeness." Lilly pushed off the desk again, spinning herself into crazy orbits. The cat on her lap tensed and then winked out again. "There, now she, *she*, Tes, not it. Now *she* is probs back in my room." She jumped up, striding over to where Tesla held an implacable Pav, who was barking at his reflection. "And at least my pet has a cool trick up her sleeve, unlike this guy. Well, there is the one." She touched a button on her communicator and a bell chimed, making Pav glitch uncontrollably. Lilly laughed, her warm golden hair trailing down her back in pigtails, hot pink streaks matching her boots. Her laughter was cut short as she caught sight of the dress. "Momma Bear still dressing you up like a china doll?"

"Lilly, did you come in here for something specific? I mean other than terrorizing my robodog and insulting me in general." Tesla narrowed her eyes at her older sister, who was feeling the fabric of the dress.

"Just came to see how product number two is faring these days. I'll leave you to … whatever it is you *do* in here." Lilly dropped the dress. "That's some lighting work. Maybe I shouldn't have fought so hard to pick out my own clothes." She looked down at her own outfit, tight neon green and black striped shorts, white tank top, hot pink faux fur shrug that matched her furry boots. She looked up at her sister with a mischievous grin. "Naw."

When she was almost at the door, she spun back to Tesla, who was still standing in the middle of the room holding a struggling Pav.

"Oh, I almost forgot, I have to ask you a teeny tiny favor."

Tesla was wary. "What is it, Lill?"

"You know tonight? The party for Skinner? Well, as much as I *long* to be there, there's an unbelievable race going down outside the Dome. I mean, this one is bigger than any I've ever seen! I just have to be there, Tes. I've even got my rig totally tricked out for it."

"You know I don't care what you do, Lill. Go take it up with Kinsey."

"I'd do that, I would, but you know how she is when she's been cooking."

"What does this have to do with me?" asked Tesla with suspicion.

"If you could just tell the parental units that I've got an awful migraine or something, anything so I can get to the race. You know that once their guests arrive, and you come in the room in *that*," she tossed her head at the gray dress, "they won't think twice about me. So just slip that in if Kinsey asks where I am."

"You know that won't work, Lill. You're an A-One. You never get sick. And you know, you shouldn't be racing out there anyways. You've already gone through more installations this year alone from accidents. With all the crazy stuff you're doing, you're going through body parts like a laser fire. Just last week you installed that arm."

"Well, why shouldn't I? Skinner can just grow me a new one anyhow." Lilly pouted, her pink bottom lip sticking out. "It's just so boring being perfect all the time! I can't take it, I need some excitement, you know?"

Tesla thought back to the afternoon, to the surge of hot blood that had flooded her normally cool cheeks as she'd watched Lynx sizzle the Evolutionist's hand off. Even thinking his name made her face warm.

Lilly crossed her arms in front of her chest. "Whatever, you wouldn't understand. You're so darn serene all the time, Dome it.

Never installed any parts." She strode toward the doorway, which slid upwards with a muted hiss.

"Wait!" Tesla glanced at an opaque oval stone laying on her desk. "I'll do it, as a favor, as long as you promise to do the same for me if I need something."

Lilly turned back, a look of astonishment making her eyes go wide.

"Whoa, wow, thanks Sis. What gives? I totally did not expect you to go for that." She cocked her head at her sister. "Sure, a favor. If you ever need anything at all, just chime me. I owe you, Tes, and if you ever need to get something off your chest ..." She wiggled her eyebrows as the smoky plastic occluded her image.

# CHAPTER FOUR

ynx could hear Below before he could see it: a swirl of human voices, singing accompanied by the twang and thump of instruments, the shouts of an argument, a baby crying. Below was essentially a honeycomb of storage units that had long ago been deemed too impractical for A-Ones to store their excess goods, being miles away from their softly colored heights. Now, however, they housed the Botches. The elevator ground to a halt in its shaft, Lynx cranked another gear on the top of the car and a door above him slid open to reveal Below.

*Why would Tesla want to come down here? Why would anyone want to come down here at all?* he thought. *It's home to me, so I love it but, man, the smell!*

Lynx slipped through the partially open doors and stepped onto a platform. The storage units stretched into narrow alleys, laid out like the spokes of a wheel sprouting from the bank of elevators. Each living unit was a long rectangle, split inside into whatever configuration best suited its occupants. The passage end was a strong plexiglass window fitted with half windows along the top.

Lynx could see into at least a dozen units, each providing its own particular slice of family life. As he walked by one he could see an elderly couple. The woman was at the sink, plunging a plate over and over into a basin of water, while the man laid an intricate card game out on a table in the light of a lantern. Lynx detoured around a group of children playing jacks on the dusty ground, some of them still unaffected by the plague. One of them called out to him and he turned, his cape swirling around him, exposing the long metal length of his left arm.

Sage, a girl of about ten, jumped up from the circle and came running over to him. She was a friend of Phlox, Lynx's little sister, but unlike Phlox, Sage had no modifications at all. She had a splash of orange hair crowning her head, sharp features and a quick smile.

"Hey there, Sage, how goes the good fight?" He held out his left arm and Sage grabbed it, swinging on it as if it were a monkey bar.

"We saw Slug and LeftEye come back. Man, they looked shaken up. What happened? I asked them where you were and they just shook their heads. Slug looked as if he were about to cry. Did something happen up there?"

Lynx glanced down the alley at the rows of plexiglass windows. "Um, yeah, something went down. We ran into an A-One. I had to strong-arm him …" Lynx paused and chuckled weakly. Sage didn't laugh. She dropped off his arm.

"What happened? How did you get away? Are you okay?" Sage's smooth forehead creased into puckers.

"Yeah, I'm fine." He tousled her hair. "Listen, why don't you come and visit Phlox tomorrow and I'll tell you all about it."

"Gotcha," the girl said, breaking into a grin and turning back to her friends. Halfway to the circle she turned back. "Hey!"

"Whassup? You forget something?"

"Bring anything back for me?"

Lynx threw his head back and guffawed. "Even when I'm risking life and limb, especially limb, you still want me to bring back a treat for you?"

"That's a 'no' then?" Sage cocked her head at him, hand on her outthrust hip.

"Better luck next time." Lynx strode down the alleyway, avoiding the bundle of electrical wires that ran next to him, and turned into the narrow hallway of number 77. A memory teased the edges of Lynx's mind like Tesla's almost-smile. He thought back to before they were adopted by Wren, before Slug had found him holding onto baby Phlox with the only arm he had left. The memory touched Lynx's mind and then shied away, as if it had been zapped by a cattle prod, skittering back to the dark corner from whence it came.

Lynx paused at the door of the pod. He could hear murmuring from within. *I bet Slug is about having a coronary*, he thought, pushing open the heavy door into the long space. The pod ran one hundred feet until it stopped at the large window that made up the final wall. Makeshift partitions had been erected at certain intervals, creating private areas for each occupant. Phlox got her own room because of her condition, Slug and Lynx shared one, and Wren had her own as well. Chick, Wren's brother, when he was in the pod and not outside the Dome, would simply wrap himself up in his jacket and sleep wherever.

The walls of the dark hallway were illuminated by the glow from the front room, where muffled voices could be heard. Slug sounded urgent and worried, compared to his mother's contralto soothing.

"He didn't make it, Wren," Slug wailed. "There's no way he got out of that mess. It was that mean A-One too, the Evolutionist."

Liquid was poured and Lynx imagined the stream of hot water falling into the teapot. "There now," Wren said. "Let this steep and drink it down. It'll calm you."

"I just wish I had done something, done something more, you know?" Slug's voice broke at the end, sounding much younger than his fifteen years.

Lynx pushed the curtain aside and strode into the room. Slug was at the kitchen table without his prosthetic legs, which leaned against the wall. Wren stood over him, stroking the back of his neck. Wren's fingers were metal but her palms still her own. Her toes, kneecaps, elbows, and both ears had been replaced. Where once had been peachy shells of small ears peeking through her salt and pepper curls, now were metal facsimiles. Whoever had made her ears seemed to have a subtle sense of humor because Wren's were pointed, and with her crackling hazel eyes and wide mouth, she resembled an elf from one of the storybooks they'd stashed at the back of the pod.

Wren looked up at the entrance of the room and, seeing it was Lynx, squeezed Slug's muscular shoulder. Slug raised his head from his hands and stared in shock at Lynx, mouth agape and brown eyes wide. Lynx slouched against the wall, pretending to check the nails of his metal hand. "Hey," he said.

"Man!" Slug said, slapping the wooden table as a grin lit up his face. "Man! You're here! How did you? I mean, how could you? Man!" He planted both palms on the table, vaulting over it with over-developed arms and his wizened lower body (his real legs came to an end just above the knees). Not disturbing the teapot's wafting steam, he swung his way over to where Lynx stood. Lynx caught him round the middle and gave him a fierce hug, then deposited him on the floor, squatting in front of him.

"How in Dome did you get loose?" Slug began. "I mean, me and LeftEye were so worried. We felt so bad, leaving you there, but when that other A-One caught you, we thought you were a goner." He grinned again, shaking his head at his foster brother. "You lucky dog!" He leaned to one side, raising his palm and high-fiving Lynx so hard it hurt.

"Come on now, let him tell his story," Wren moved to where Lynx stood, tears standing out in her already-bright eyes. "We're awfully glad to see you," she said, giving him a quick squeeze. "Sit down and tell us everything. I'll get you a mug."

Lynx sat down at the wooden table, scarred from many meals and long nights whiled away with friends. Wren swiped at her eyes and turned to a bank of cupboards. She plunked three mismatched, chipped mugs on the table and poured a long stream of fragrant liquid into each. Slug swung himself back into his original seat as Wren sat down across from him.

Lynx took a sip of the tea, letting the cinnamon-flavored liquid wash down his throat. "Well," he began. As he recounted their experience in the bazaar, the look on Wren's face changed from shock, to surprise, to awe. As Lynx reached the point when he blasted Darwin's hand off, Wren leaned back in her seat, a low whistle coming from parted lips. "Wow, his whole hand? The plague that's taking our body parts doesn't seem to affect those A-Ones at all, maybe this is a bit of payback." She tapped a silver fingertip on Lynx's metal arm, the sound like a raindrop falling onto a tin drum. "You helped Slug get away, but how did you escape?"

"An A-One, a girl." Lynx's face took on a dreamy quality. Wren and Slug exchanged glances across the table.

"A what now?" Slug asked, eyebrows raised.

"An A-One, Tesla, she stopped them."

"She just … stopped them from vaporizing you?" Wren said.

"Yeah, I was on my knees, and he had the tube right here, pointing at my eye, when she stopped him."

"Lynx," Wren said. "A-Ones don't do that for us. They don't just step in and stop us from getting hurt. Why would she do that?"

"I don't know," Lynx said. "She said that she was intrigued by my loyalty and bravery."

"You … talked to her."

Lynx nodded.

"Did she get you to promise her anything, Lynx?" Wren's voice filled with urgency. "Anything at all?"

Lynx opened his mouth to speak and then closed it, torn between his allegiance to the family who'd taken him and his sister in, and to the girl who had most recently saved his life. "I ... she ..." he stuttered, opening and closing his metal fist. "She asked me to ..."

The electrical system suddenly went down with an audible whine. Out the window, lights blinked off up and down the alley like fireflies. Relief surged through Lynx.

Wren swore and stood up from the table, jostling it. She fumbled to the sink and found a lantern. As she worked the hand crank at its side, she barked orders at the two boys. "Slug, you go tell Phlox not to worry. Lynx, I know you just got here but you're going to have to get us back on-line tonight, so head out there and see if anything can be done with the wiring. Those A-Ones," she spat, as a small incandescent light bloomed in the glass enclosure, throwing her cheekbones into sharp relief. "Someone up there must've found out we were sipping off their electric and didn't like it."

Lynx heard Slug thumping down the hall, calling "Phlox?" Lynx moved to Wren's side and reached into the upper cupboards, pulling down a headlamp, a canteen, and a package of rations, as well as a compressed blanket. As he was stuffing these into a small pack, Wren placed a hand on his shoulder. It was a strange sensation, the feeling of her warm palm and her cold metal fingertips.

"This girl," Wren started. "What did she look like?"

Lynx occupied himself with putting the items in the pack with deliberate care. "Um," he began, stalling. "She's an A-One so she's, you know, perfect."

"Yeah, I got that much, but what does she specifically look like?"

"All pale and stuff, light eyes, light hair, light skin. She wore this silver shimmery gown too, I think it had something done to it so that it would float."

Wren took her hand off Lynx's shoulder and began tapping nervously on the basin that served as their sink. "Yeah, they have those made specially so that they don't get Underdweller grime on their beautiful clothes. I'm sure they burn them afterward when they get back up there." Wren's gaze went past Lynx, to somewhere else. Suddenly, she focused on him again. "Lynx, I need you to promise me something."

*Jeez, twice in one day?* "What is it?"

"That you won't get involved with her, no matter what she tries to get you to do. I have a terrible feeling about this. Did she tell you her production code?"

Lynx thought back to Tesla's conversation with Darwin. "She said something like X321? Or was it X723?"

Wren inhaled. "Do you mean X3721?"

"Yes! That was it! I'm like 85% sure that was her code. She called herself Tesla though."

Wren was shaking her head. "Oh, by Dome, you had to get saved by the highest ranking A-One there is. And now you're on a first name basis. I do not like this. I sure wish Chick was here." Wren's tapping sped up as she gazed off into an imaginary distance again. Lynx shuffled in front of her, holding onto the pack and digging through his brain for an excuse to leave. From down the hall, a young girl's voice called, "Lynx?"

Lynx jerked his head toward the hall and moved around Wren. As he passed, she put her hand once again on his shoulder. "Please Lynx, please don't get involved with her any more than you have to."

Lynx stood quietly for a few seconds, then nodded. Making his way down the darkened hallway and feeling along the walls until he reached a doorway, Lynx could make out Slug and another figure sitting up in bed by the faint glow of a lantern.

"Hey Sis, how're you feeling?"

Phlox ignored the question from her perch amidst what looked to be all the blankets in the pod. Her small face peered out of a forest of jet-black curls. Her green eyes glowed in the lantern light. "Sluggo here was filling me in on what happened. Gosh Lynx, I'm sure glad you're okay."

Lynx walked over to the bed and leaned over, gathering up Phlox with his human arm and squeezing her close. He could feel her hair against his neck and her sweet breath on his cheek. A small whine of pain escaped her lips; Lynx let go.

"Oh hey, I'm sorry, did I hurt you at all?"

Phlox smoothed the coverlet over her legs, her wavy hair covering her eyes for a moment. When she lifted her face to her brother's, she pushed her hair back and smiled at him. "All set, don't you worry. I'm not quite used to the newest change yet. It was just last week. Chick says I'll be right as rain-time in no time at all." She stretched out her arm in wonder. "That darn plague sure has it in for me."

Lynx's throat constricted and he half turned away, saying, "Listen I've got to go get us on-line. I'll be back before you know it." At the doorway, he turned back, "I saw Sage down at the platform. She said she'd come for a visit tomorrow."

From her bed, Phlox kept her brother fixed with her eyes. "That'll be great. It'll be nice to see her." She cocked her head at him, and Lynx, remembering the same posture on the perfect Tesla, strode out of the room before his sister could glimpse the expression on his face.

# CHAPTER FIVE

To get their pod back on-line, Lynx had far to travel. He'd be back later in the evening, but he'd brought emergency rations just in case he got stuck out there. He was headed for the outer edge of the Dome, and this wasn't the cultivated part of the Dome edging the bazaar in Middlespace. This was the backside of the Dome, the forgotten area, the twists of cords and wires that, if still fully functional, didn't need untangling. He preferred to get there as quickly as possible and avoided the crowded surface by traveling underground using the sewers, finding his way back up when he reached the outer point of his destination.

The Botches referred to these massive pipes as the Waterworks, although Lynx figured they did this to forget the fact that they were traveling the same paths as their own waste. The A-Ones piped out their waste themselves, not deigning to mix even their excrement with that of the lower orders. The waste from Above caught up with that from Below, whether they admitted it or not, at the outskirts of the Dome, two tubes merging into one gigantic river of nastiness. Then it was shot out into the atmosphere, where the superstorms and giant tornados dispersed the stream of putrefaction better than any waste treatment center could.

A lot of the gray water in the Dome, the water from dishwashing and cleaning up in general, was purified and reused. But raw sewage took too much time and energy to sanitize, and so the only solution seemed to be to void it completely. Out of sight, out of mind. It also seemed like a not too subtle way to shove it to the outside environment that was mostly uninhabitable. If humans couldn't survive outside the Dome for long, they could certainly show their displeasure at the situation by spraying the offending environment with their own waste.

Lynx hooked up the harness that ran along the ceiling of the tunnel. Two straps under and around his shoulders, another two looping his groin. He buckled them across his chest and ratcheted himself up until he was swaying fifteen feet above, looking at the sodden floor of the waste pipe. He dug in his pocket for a nose clamp, inserted it and, breathing through his mouth, pulled down yellow-tinted goggles to keep out the fumes. Rolling up the long sleeve of his jumpsuit, Lynx exposed his modified arm. He twisted a lever near the wrist, aiming it into the maw of darkness in front of him, and released the hand, trusting it to use its own innate ability to find purchase. The arm, Chick had explained, was something of a "smart arm." Although not capable of independent action—*Dome, that would be freaky*—it was able to accomplish simple tasks. For example, right now it would find a suitable place to grip far ahead of Lynx. A muted clang echoed through the tunnel and Lynx felt the tremor through the braided cables of his wrist.

He twisted the dial to the left, and the retraction jerked him as he released the break on the harness. The oiled wheels running along the cable above him slid up to speed as Lynx opened the throttle up. Cross-sections of tunnels threading into the heart of Dome life whipped by his goggled eyes, and soon they blurred into one continuous streak of light. Legs straight out behind him, modified arm stretching into the darkness ahead of him, Lynx was a horizontal human arrow. After a few minutes of controlled hurtling through the tunnel shaft, Lynx reached up and dialed back on his modified arm, slowing his forward motion until he could read the string of numbers crowning each tunnel.

"415, 416, 417," Lynx read aloud until he reached a tunnel that read 420 and twisted the dial on his arm, swaying in his harness with the sudden lack of forward motion. As he pivoted in the air, still suspended fifteen feet above the thick brown river of putridness, he tapped buttons on his robotic arm and felt the immediate pull as his hand retracted. The cables in the inner workings of his arm were stiff enough, coupled with powerful magnets embedded in both hand and wrist, to allow for a retraction without the hand dragging through the muck below him. A glint in the darkness announced its arrival; a few seconds more it had found the wrist port with a magnetic clink. Unhitching the harness, Lynx pulled himself to the opening of the tunnel and fixed both hands onto the rung of a ladder that led up toward a circle of violet light at the very top. With a grunt, he started to climb.

By the time Lynx reached it, he was sweaty and red-faced. He pulled himself up and over the lip, straightening up for the first time on his journey. He was in a crowded circular room. Beyond a mass of thick wires and electrical conductors was the edge of the Dome, transparent but pock-marked from the constant stinging spray of the sand outside. Night was just falling, and a red band limned the distant sharp shapes of mountains as well as the bulbous forms of the smaller domes out on the Rim.

Lynx stood for a few moments, feeling the coldness of the outside environment through the thick skin of the Dome. It was a moment of clear weather. There were a few of these each day, a span of thirty minutes or so when the howling winds and deadly eddy of tornadoes ceased. Lynx pushed back from the large window and set to work on the electrical grid before him. He hummed to himself as he worked, unaware that he was doing so. Opening up a compartment embedded in his forearm, Lynx laid out the tools he would need to redistribute current back Below. As he had on the elevator, he opened up the tip of his pointer finger and clicked a switch, the top of his missing finger suddenly emitting a blue glow. Lynx applied it to the thick wires before him, all the time checking the connections and replacing them when they seemed as if they'd been fried.

*It looks as if there was another surge,* Lynx thought as small sparks pinged around his concentrated face. *It sure seems as if the A-Ones are onto us stealing their energy. I don't understand why they don't just cut the system completely, instead of surging it every once and a while. Not that I'm complaining. At least this way we get the juice.* Once he had checked and replaced every connection to the grid, he started to work on the bigger bundles of cables feeding into it. Finally, he clanged a large lever to the left and the static hum of current reverberated throughout the tunnel. *That should do it,* he thought, replacing the tools back into his arm. *And that's why I get paid the big bucks.*

He broke open his rations, taking out some hard tack and the small thermos of water. Even though he could've gotten back in time for the evening meal, he remained, using the solitude to think over Wren's words about Tesla.

*The highest ranking A-One,* he thought while chewing the tough biscuit. *That would explain the other A-Ones' reaction to her. I wonder if it was a bad idea, agreeing to bring her Below.* He reached into the small pouch that he wore and, for a moment, held the oval stone Tesla had given him. It was cold and smooth. *Just like her skin.* His face heated up at the thought of touching her. *That is an absolute impossibility,* he admonished. *That can never be, so don't even go there. Never ever.* His name echoed up from the narrow tunnel, surprising him. *Slug,* he thought.

"Lynx? Are you in here?"

Another voice piped up, one that Lynx knew very well indeed. "Maybe he's on his way back."

*Phlox!* Lynx strode over to the circular opening just as Phlox's head came into view, followed closely by Slug. Phlox gripped Slug's back as he strained to get both their bodies over the lip. Lynx reached over and Phlox, smiling up at him, clamped her hand on his metal arm as he pulled her off his friend's back. She continued grinning into his scowling face as she swung back and forth in front of him.

"What?" She asked, all innocence and raised eyebrows.

"You know what," he growled back, scooping her close and setting her with care on a breaker box next to the glass skin of the Dome.

"What in Dome's name are you two doing here?" Lynx didn't wait for an answer. "Actually, strike that, what is *she* doing here, Slug?"

"Lynx," Phlox started but he put a hand up behind him to silence her, staring at Slug frozen in front of him.

"What were you thinking, Slug? She's in a fragile state right now. She could've really gotten hurt."

Slug looked at the metal feet protruding from his yellow coveralls. "I know, Lynx, I'm sorry. She made me do it! I didn't have a choice. You know, she can be really convincing."

"Yeah, I made him take me here, Lynx, please don't be mad at him." Phlox's voice rose plaintively. "I haven't see the outside in so long and I needed to talk to you ... OOOH!"

Lynx spun around. Phlox had lifted one small hand to the inside of the Dome, staring with undisguised delight at the view opening up before her. The red glow still lit the mountain range in the distance, and now the last purply rays of the sun hit the ring of outer domes, lighting each one up like the buttons on a pinball machine.

"It's so beautiful," her voice was edged in awe. Lynx's fury drained away as he watched her face, vivid with joy and the last rays of the sunset. He walked over and touched the small of her back, feeling the plates of metal interwoven beneath the thin clothing.

She turned toward him, her dark eyes alive with the night fire outside. "Tell me about her," she asked.

Lynx waited a beat, too used to his sister's direct manner to be unnerved by it much. "Who?" He asked.

Phlox swatted him on the shoulder.

"Ouch!" he said, rubbing at the spot. "Quit it, you're too strong for your own good, you know?"

A faint smile played around the edges of Phlox's mouth as she stroked the fabric of her brown corduroy trousers. "No, really," she said, pleading eyes staring into his. "What's she like?"

Lynx dropped his hand. "She's beautiful."

Phlox nodded, turning her head once again to the outside world. The sun had fully set and a storm was building to the west, blocking out the mountains and moving toward them, the billowing black clouds rolling over the barren landscape like a malevolent jellyfish.

"We need to see if my fix worked," Lynx said, starting for the mouth of the tunnel. "And you need to get back to bed. The last time was only a few days ago, Phlox."

"I bet they're all beautiful," Phlox leaned forward until her forehead pressed against the inside of the Dome, metal hands starfished on either side of her pale face. "Hey Lynx? Why don't you ever talk about what happened before we were with Wren?" She shifted her head so that she could look at him.

"I don't remember, Phlox. You know that. I've told you that before."

"You have to remember something about what came before." A crease formed between her straight brows. "Something, anything?"

Lynx shook his head, holding his hands out in supplication.

Phlox snorted and turned her head back to the view as the first spit of sand lashed the Dome. They couldn't see the outlying ring of smaller domes now, the thick angry clouds blacked them out.

"I wish I was the older one," she said. "I would remember everything."

# CHAPTER SIX

T he sounds of the dinner party wafted toward Tesla as she came down the hallway toward the living room. The gray material shimmered and rustled around her as the lights pulsed gently, her own bioelectricity fueling them. She took a deep breath at the threshold of the room, touching the headband she'd twisted through her hair, folding the hair and the fabric into a large bun atop her head. She entered the oval living room, making her way past the pale sofas to a group of seven people gathered at the bank of windows that looked over the sparkling diorama of Middlespace all the way to the edge of the Dome, and beyond to the vast darkness of the wilderness outside.

Her father was the first one to notice her. Skinner, at sixty-five, was an ideal specimen of an A-One. He was tall, and his bald head shone with the special oil he used on it. He was dressed, as usual, in a crisp white collarless shirt and pressed gray pants. Loafers and a slim silver watch were his only accessories.

"Tesla, you're a vision," he stated matter-of-factly. "Ladies and gentleman, I'd like you to meet the most perfect one of us all: my daughter, Tesla."

The circle opened up and appreciative murmurs rippled through the guests. Tesla hated this feeling of being paraded around like a Blue Ribbon poodle, but she nodded and smiled to those guests she knew, introducing herself with a curtsey to those she didn't. Kinsey, her hair a cotton candy poof and her decolletage on full display, squeezed Tesla's shoulder as she passed, whispering, "Gorgeous."

Soon she had met and greeted everyone and was back at her father's side. Skinner held a glass of a softly bubbling beverage. Tesla suspected it was not his first of the evening as she listened to him hold court with stories from the lab, his electronic pipe blinking blue as he periodically drew on its stem. Kinsey was on his right, nodding and smiling. As he was chortling about mixing a crucial solution, which had come close to resulting in disaster, a chime sounded from behind them. The mech maid stood in the entrance to the dining room, LED candles flickering behind it.

"Dinner, Ma'am," the mech maid directed at Kinsey, rolling back out of sight on wheels disguised under its black and white "formal" outfit. Kinsey clapped her hands, gushing to the woman on her right, who was dressed in yellow silk pajamas and whose black bob was cut severely at the jawline, how Kinsey herself had cooked this meal "from scratch."

*That's why she cooked it, instead of programming Carver and the kitchen to do it. Now she can brag,* Tesla thought as she followed her mother into the dining room.

The guests were soon arranged around the onyx dining table, which was set with white plates and napkins, the only splash of color some fake coral peonies in a vase at the center. As soon as everyone had settled into their chairs, Kinsey nodded at the mech maid, who resembled a human except that its translucent skin showed the pulsing wires underneath. Immediately, outlines of circles appeared under each plate and they descended into the table. In a moment, they reappeared loaded with the first course, a cold salad. For A-Ones, presentation and aesthetic effect were valued as much if not more than taste. Cubes of bright green pureed peas were served with a dollop of pesto, three asparagus the size of toothpicks sprouting from each.

The guests oohed and aahed. Tesla had to admit the colors were quite beautiful against the white plates and black table. Two more discs depressed in the table and a pitcher of the pale pink bubbling liquid as well as one of deep garnet red appeared. Skinner grabbed for a pitcher and filled his glass to the rim. Kinsey shot him a quick glance and turned back to a small man with an impressive moustache and spectacles, which he wore only for effect, since all A-Ones had 20-20 vision.

The first course finished, the plates once again disappeared from view only to be replaced by dishes of miniature potatoes resembling pearls, and crickets the size of lobsters sitting atop them.

"Oooh cricket!" The black-haired woman exclaimed, leaning over her plate and waving her hands to better waft the aroma to her flared nostrils. "My absolute favorite. What a marvelous spread you have put before us, Kinsey!"

Kinsey inclined her head and reached across the table for Skinner's hand. "It's not every day my partner gets a promotion to be top programmer."

"Now, now," Skinner admonished. "It hasn't been announced yet. Don't jinx it," he said, dropping Kinsey's hand and ripping a leg off his cricket.

The bespectacled man was heaping potatoes on his fork with his knife. "How will your position be any different than what you do now, Skinner? I mean if you do get the promotion, which I am sure you will," he amended.

Skinner looked around at his collected colleagues and grinned, winking at Tesla. "Well, you know I don't really like talking about myself but …" Kinsey tittered and was hushed by a look from Skinner.

Skinner picked up his glass, sloshing the garnet liquid within.

"I like to think of it this way," he began, studying his drink. "Before, what I did was to look inward, inside the Dome. I, along with a few choice others, made sure that the infrastructure was sound and running smoothly." Tesla inwardly groaned as her father picked up momentum.

"But now," his eyes widened as he glanced from guest to guest, "Now I am looking outward, to the stars, to beyond. Whereas before I was constantly monitoring the stasis of the environment within our Dome, now I will be working with forces outside of it, creating a presence for our society in the grand scheme of things. Suffice it to say, before I maintained perfect order out of the chaos within us, but now I seek to create a balance between us ... and whatever exists out there." He raised his fluted glass in the air, looking expectantly as each guest raised theirs in turn, taking a moment to clink rims.

Tesla, sensing her opportunity, waited for the company to replace their glasses on the table before turning her attention to her father. "But Skinner, who exactly are you working for?"

Skinner gazed at Tesla for a few beats, a sly smile on his lips. "Not quite enough information to satisfy you, X3721? No surprise there." He turned to his guests. "Out of my two girls, Tesla here never lets anything get by her. Lilly is ... energetic to say the least, and you can't tell that one what to do, not a bit. She'll do the opposite just to spite you. But Tesla here, she is a still pool, but very deep." Skinner fixed his gaze on Tesla. "Perceptive as well as beautiful, an intriguing mix of qualities."

Tesla squirmed under the appreciative gaze of the table, wondering if perhaps this was Skinner's way of repaying her pointed question, as he knew how private she was.

"And," Skinner continued, pinning her to her seat with a look, "if I was to tell you for whom I work, it would incur drastic consequences. So I cannot, not yet."

A silence fell on the table like a fog, despite Kinsey's aborted attempts to restart the conversation. It was only when the dessert course had been offered up, a mound of tiny cream-puffs in a pyramid glazed with threads of caramel so fine they looked like sparkling strands of hair, that normal conversation continued. Skinner let the issue drop with only a few more glances Tesla's way. After the guests adjourned to the living room with coffees in hands, Skinner took Tesla's shoulder, holding her back from joining the party.

"And what was that all about?" He growled, his tanned face folding in displeasure.

"I ... I'm just curious about what you do, Skinner. Is that alright?" Her voice was stronger than she felt.

"No actually, it's not. Your duty until you are launched is to be a still pool: smart, obedient and beautiful to look at. Not inquisitive and willful. I can't correct those particular traits in your sister, not anymore, but she's not quite clever enough to ask the right questions. You on the other hand ..." He paused, watching her squirm under his searing gaze. "I believe I've made myself clear." With that he stretched his face into a grin and walked out of the room to join his guests.

Tesla took a moment to compose herself, moving napkins and used cutlery to the plates. The mech maid rolled around her, shooing her away from the table. Tesla straightened up and adjusted her dress, planning on walking unnoticed across the living room and hopefully to her room. She thought with envy of Lilly, partying it up at some club, racing across the desert with her friends, bunjee jumping off the tallest spires of the Dome. Halfway through the room, Kinsey's voice rang out and Tesla cringed.

"Tes darling, come and see the magnificent showing of stars! The storm has ceased for the moment. We can even see the moon."

Tesla turned back from her beckoning hallway to the group

gathered at the windows. Sure enough, she could see an orange crescent moon hanging over the darkened landscape like a slice of melon. Her ears perked up as she heard the man with the moustache mention "Underdwellers" from where he stood with Skinner.

"It's impossible that we will be able to maintain this," he was saying. "Sooner or later there will be a revolt."

"Nonsense! They're incapable of an uprising. A calculated move so that they don't overreact to ... anything. You know that they're emotionless, at least they don't have any strong emotions that count."

"That's not true!" Tesla exclaimed, interrupting the casual conversations around them. The guests stopped and turned toward her. Kinsey pulled at her necklace.

"They can feel, they have loyalty. I know it! For a fact!" She couldn't stop the words even as Skinner's face reddened.

"And how did you come across this information, Tesla?" her father asked in a very quiet voice.

Tesla swallowed audibly, her mind whirring to find a suitable response. "I ... I ... I saw one, in the garden you and Kinsey sponsored, and he was ... talking to his friend."

The collected A-Ones gasped.

"You didn't talk to them, did you Tesla?" Skinner moved a step toward her and Tesla reflexively stepped back.

"No ... no," she stammered. "They ran when they caught sight of me." She could see the hollowness of her words hanging before her.

Kinsey blew out the air she had been holding in. "Well, that's a relief. And what were you doing in Middlespace by yourself?" Kinsey was agitated, her hands on her hips and her small foot tapping in a patent leather flat.

"I was bored up here one afternoon. So I went down to look around."

Kinsey came close to her, placing a hand on her shoulder and looking into her eyes. "Tes, I know that you're smart and maybe all this," she waved her hand at the room, "can get tedious at times. But that's not safe!"

Seeing the distress in her mother's eyes, Tesla felt a pang of guilt and lowered her head. "I know, I'm sorry, parental producer."

"Product number two, it's my job to take care of you before you are out on your own. And as I made you, I feel a small responsibility for your well-being."

Tesla looked up at Kinsey through webbed lashes to see her mother half-smiling, trying to diffuse the tension. Around them, guests feebly chatted while watching the pair out of the corners of their eyes. Tesla winked and swept a large curtsey. Kinsey clapped as the lights embedded in Tesla's dress lit up.

"If it's alright with you, I'll be retiring for the evening." Tesla said, head still inclined.

"Yes, Tesla, I think that you've been illuminating enough this evening," Skinner said smiling, although the smile did not reach his eyes as he watched her.

Tesla bid goodbye to the various guests and headed toward the hallway.

"Oh Tes?" Her mother's voice trailed after her. She whirled, the lights spinning with her. "Where's your sister tonight?"

Tesla clasped her hands behind her back, fingers on both hands crossed. "She's studying at Sagan's house. Astronomy." *Keep it short and sweet.*

Kinsey nodded and turned back to her conversation but Skinner continued staring at Tesla until the woman in yellow diverted his attention again.

Minutes later Tesla sat in bed with Pav snoring at her feet, glitching on every exhalation. Her new dress glowed in her closet. In her hand she held a stone, a match to the one she had given Lynx earlier. She ran her fingers over the smooth shape. Bringing it to her mouth, she breathed on it, clouding its charcoal surface. With the tip of her pinky finger, she traced the necessary symbol on it and the stone began to pulse, illuminating Tesla's soft smile.

"Tomorrow," she whispered, tucking it under her pillow.

# CHAPTER SEVEN

An hour before dawn, with Tesla asleep high above them, Lynx and LeftEye were on their way back to the Dome from the outer Rim where they'd made off with their weekly supplies, unchallenged. The boat was tearing across the floor of the desert at breakneck speed with LeftEye at the helm as usual. His pulsing red eye beamed through the darkness, searching for the access point where they would re-enter the Dome. The sails were furled in the dark of pre-dawn because their ship had amassed enough solar power in the previous days as it waited, camouflaged, buffeted by wind, rain, and violent tornadoes.

Lynx was harnessed on the trapeze, or the trap, toes hooked over the edge of the boat, flying parallel to the ground. In the forward hold were three sacks of assorted foodstuffs and two large water casks that held enough for both their families for a week. Lynx looked beyond LeftEye and grimaced, gauging the distance between their small craft and the approaching set of storms. The dark clouds rolled over the landscape, obscuring the view of the ring of smaller supply domes they'd just left. Bulbous and angry, the clouds were gaining on them.

The wind tore the words out of Lynx's mouth when he attempted to speak, so he waved at LeftEye to get his attention, pointing at the approaching storm. LeftEye glanced behind them and then turned back to the Dome, cloak streaking out behind him, hand on the power stick, inching it forward until it was all out.

In the final approach, Lefteye swung the tiller hard to port, spinning the boat and letting it drift on its wheels sideways toward the thick expanse of the Dome reaching above them. The approaching storm reflected in the Dome's surface, making it seem as if they were surrounded by treacherous weather. LeftEye hurled a chain attached to a round ball off the stern. It arced toward the dusty ground, disengaging its many hooks as it landed. The dense strands burrowed into the earth, embedding the anchor firmly into the hard surface. LeftEye raced to the bow of the boat for the second and third anchor as Lynx heaved the sacks of food off and leapt down, worriedly glancing around as the first fierce winds tugged at his clothing and hair.

"Come on!" he yelled into the rising howl. LeftEye handed down the two jugs of water and threw a camouflaged cover up and over the boat, hooking it into grommets as he went. Lynx was waiting with a cart piled high with the supplies. He began to push it towards the access port even before LeftEye had finished, sand stinging his cheeks like a slap. LeftEye leapt off and sprinted after him as the boat was overtaken by a whistling sandstorm. Lynx reached the edge of the Dome, typing the code into the access port with haste and manhandling the overladen cart into the space beyond. The only way he knew that LeftEye was still coming was the glowing red eye in the churning texture of flung sand.

The bobbing red spot disappeared, black clouds swirling around the figure until all that was left was sand and dirt and angry, angry wind. *C'mon Lefty, get lucky tonight!* Lynx thought, pounding the cart's handle with his metal fist hard enough to dent it and squinting his eyes against the sand. He waited, reading the wall of furious weather as it rapidly approached him. His hand toyed with the button that would close the access door and leave LeftEye to fend for himself in the swirling maelstrom. Just as he was about to push it, the red light reappeared. LeftEye skidded inside the port, a pile of cloak and dirt as Lynx punched the button and the doors slid shut, leaving them in silence as the storm roared revenge outside. Lynx typed in numbers as LeftEye choked and coughed on the metal flooring. The pressure took hold with a *schink*. LeftEye looked up, grit covering his face.

"That," he said, grinning with dirt-covered teeth, "was most awesome."

Lynx laughed as he helped his friend to his feet, clouds of dirt and sand billowing off his clothes. "You sure know how to make an entrance."

"It's a natural talent," LeftEye agreed, wiping his cheek.

The two turned to face the inner door as it slid open. Before them stretched a dark tunnel, unused carts lining the hallway.

LeftEye spoke up as they reached a platform before the bank of elevators. "You never did tell me how you got away from the A-One."

Lynx paused as he cranked the elevator doors open. "Oh, I um, I lucked out."

LeftEye just stared at him, his mild brown eye urging Lynx to say more.

"There was this girl, an A-One. She stood up for me."

"Well hey," LeftEye said, entering numbers into the code board. "I've never heard of that ever happening. An A-One saved you? Why would she do that?"

"She said it was because I stepped in when Slug was about to get it from that red-headed A-One. She said she didn't think that Botches had loyalty to one another and that I surprised her."

"You talked to her," LeftEye's human eye went wide, almost as wide as his artificial one.

"Yeah," Lynx bragged. "And she gave me this." As they slid

downward, he fumbled at his waistline for his leather pouch, pulling out the stone Tesla had given him and holding it up for his friend to see. To Lynx's surprise, it was pulsing with light and a slight vibration.

"Jeez, that's a pretty bauble. What's it do?" LeftEye reached out to touch it, but Lynx dropped it back into his pouch.

"Nothing," he mumbled. "It's just something to remind me of … my close call." He turned his face away from his friend as they glided downwards, calculating just how much time it would take him to get back up to the surface.

After delivering LeftEye and his portion of supplies to his pod, Lynx headed back to his own home with the sack of food and a water casket dangling around his shoulders. *I'll need to tell them something and NOT that I'm going to meet up with Tesla,* Lynx thought and then scowled. He took a deep breath and turned down his alley. To his surprise, the door to his pod was open, flooding the usually dark passageway with warm light. He heard Wren laugh, and then a chuckle he instantly recognized. He ran the last few feet, dropping their supplies at the entrance, and bounded into the room, a grin already stretching his features.

Wren was moving around the worn table, where Phlox, looking pale but happy, sat next to Slug. A large man with his back to Lynx was telling a story, gesturing as he spoke. Wren looked up at Lynx, her dark eyes gleaming, looking every inch an elf. "Lynx! Look who just got back!"

"Chick!" he shouted. The big man rose and turned as Lynx enveloped him in a bear hug.

"Easy," Chick said, pulling away. "That arm's strong. I should know, I put it on you myself." The two regarded each other, Chick's dark golden curls had grown longer and his face, although leathery and weary from the long hours in the harsh environment outside the Dome, glowed with happiness as he looked the younger man over. "Well, boy-o, you're looking right as rain. And that arm?" Lynx offered up his appendage and Chick turned it over in his broad hands. "No glitches?" Lynx shook his head emphatically. "Figured out all its tricks yet?"

Lynx shook his head, looking in wonder at his arm.

"Open up the top hatch there, the one I put in last time."

Lynx flipped open the compartment on the top of his arm. Chick reached in and slid a small panel on the inside wall of the arm, revealing a blinking light.

"This will act as a homing device. Wherever you are, I'll know it. And I'll respond as quickly as I can. Now this next addition is going to blow your socks off." Lynx took another look at the light and then slid the panel back into place. "Dislocate your hand for me there."

Lynx complied, twisting the hand off and revealing the grappling hook as well as the laser.

"Now, in your wrist," Chick grabbed hold of Lynx's wrist and twisted a band, like a bracelet, clockwise. "You have another set of tools and weapons at your disposal. One of them is a levitation ray, and another is a cryogenic ray that will freeze objects or people."

Lynx looked from his arm to his uncle in awe.

"Try it out, this one here is the levitation ray."

Lynx pointed his wrist at a chair across the room. A purple ray jumped from it and enveloped the chair with purple webbing. Lifting his arm, he could feel an unnatural tugging as if he were carrying something that was balancing on a very long pole. Slowly, across the room, the chair lifted until it was seven feet in the air.

"Genius!" Lynx exclaimed, taking his attention off the chair for a moment and looking at Chick.

"Don't—" was all Chick could get out before the chair clattered to the ground, the purple webbing retracting back up into Lynx's arm with an elastic snap. "You'll need to work on that one but here's a hint: in order to keep it aloft, you need to keep your concentration on the object, or person," Chick said with a sly wink.

"Gotcha, concentrate," Lynx said, reattaching his hand to his forearm and sitting down as Wren plunked a steaming mug in front of him. "Totally awesome."

"I was just telling these guys the latest while you were out getting supplies. Hey Lynx, thanks for being the one to do that. I owe you," Chick said.

Embarrassed, Lynx raised the mug to his lips.

"Big things are happening out there, guys. Big big changes are happening," Chick continued with his story. There was a whoosh as Wren lit a burner, moving a fry pan over the tiny blue flame with a clang. "Most of the time I'm scavenging for extra parts, you all know that. Well, I hit the jackpot. There is a facility out there, beyond the outer domes, under the surface. It's truly amazing, I don't know what it was used for, or when, but I'm figuring it out."

Lynx listened as he sipped his tea. Chick's pack was balanced on one of the mismatched armchairs. The goggles that he wore outside were hanging by one of the straps, their infrared lenses pulsing like jewels.

"It's huge down there, and pretty well-kept for some place that's been abandoned. At times, I'm not even that sure that it *is* abandoned, but that's for later. There's so much metal, so many parts. If we salvaged it all we would never have to worry about coming up with more parts again."

Wren put a plate of steaming food in front of her brother. "You can't be serious," she admonished as she handed over a fistful of utensils.

"Thanks Sis, and I am. Very serious. It's really unbelievable," he said through a mouthful. "Thing is, I don't know if I want to salvage the metal until I'm sure of what it's for. Although we need all we can get at the rate that we're being used up by that plague." His face took on a serious pall as he considered Lynx and then Slug. "Anything new have to be put on you?"

Lynx shook his head as did Slug.

"Good, that makes two of you," Chick said with feeling. "Darn plague," he said as he regarded Phlox who was very small and very still across the table. "You'd think the A-Ones would've come up with a cure for it by now."

At the mention of the A-Ones, Lynx started in his chair, sloshing burning liquid onto his human hand. *Oh Dome, what time is it?* he thought.

"What's up, Lynx?" Wren asked.

"Oh, I forgot in the excitement that I was going to help out a friend. And I still have to unload all those supplies for you …" He trailed off, standing and looking at the discarded sacks by the door.

Chick wiped his broad mouth and flapped his hand at Lynx. "Listen boy-o, I'll take care of all that today. You go meet your *friend*." He drew out the word, waggling his eyebrows at Lynx until the teenager blushed, "and I'll hold down the fort here. Go on, you deserve it. You work hard for this family."

Lynx glanced at Wren who smiled and nodded at him. "We've got it all handled, Lynx. Go have a little fun with your friend." She giggled and Lynx moaned. "Especially after what you did for Slug yesterday." Her tone was serious again. "Go on."

As Lynx headed down the hallway, he heard Chick ask, "What do you mean what he did for Slug?"

The last Lynx could hear was Wren starting the story, "Well, Slug had an A-One after him, almost got him too …"

Then Lynx was out the door. It was only when he was atop the elevator, shooting for the surface for the second time that day, that he realized that he wasn't just going to go see Tesla. He was about to bring an A-One Below.

# CHAPTER EIGHT

The garden looked different this time: an ominous air hung over the bubble of tranquility. Lynx was panting from his hustle from the elevators and through the bazaar, not exactly running through the various vendors but not strolling either. All the way, he had been wondering what to *do* with Tesla once he got her down Below. Would she want to meet the family? *I hope to Dome she doesn't because I'll refuse.* Tesla's crystalline profile floated through his mind, a ghost of a smile hovering around the corners of her mouth. *But will I be able to say no to her?*

Glancing around the green space, Lynx saw no sign of the pretty A-One with the wash of light hair. He took a moment to slow his frantic breathing, straightening his shirt and brushing his human hand through his disheveled hair. Abandoning his search for Tesla for a moment, he dipped his hand into the onyx pool below the fountain, watching the petals that were scattered across the surface swirl in the eddies that he created. *Kind of like what the A-Ones do to us Botches. One touch and we're reeling.*

A discreet cough came from behind him. He stood up, whirling, but still no figure came forward.

"Tesla?" he called, searching the hanging vines and marble columns for a hint of movement. "Are you there?"

There was a moment when the air in the garden was still,

52

frozen in fact, and then Tesla stepped out from behind the farthest column. She had dressed the part in loden-colored denim pants, distressed enough not to look brand new. On top she wore a loose tunic of a similar color that was cinched in at her waist with a wide belt, also distressed on purpose. Her hair was covered with a brown cap shaped to her skull and coming to a point in the middle of her forehead, like a widow's peak. It was loose enough around the bottom edge so that her two long braids could escape to trail down to the bottom of her ribcage. She was toying with the end of one of her pigtails as she approached, her leather boots flashing in the dim light. When she reached him, she stopped and opened her mouth to say something, but thought better of it and closed it, resembling one of the fake guppies in the pool by their side.

"Hi," Lynx said, breaking the ice. He stuck his hand out in front of him, regretting the gesture as soon as he had done it.

Tesla took his hand in her cold one, ducking her head a little as she shook his hand. "Hi."

It was only when she was this close that Lynx saw her true disguise. The side of her face had been painted with special makeup. Around her eye and across her temple, disappearing into her hair, were wires painted in shimmering grays and blacks. Beads, glowing like water droplets, followed the arc of her brow. The whole impression was that of a person who'd had the left side of her head, her eye even, replaced by metal.

Lynx gave a low whistle. "Look at you, Miss Tesla," he said. "You've gone and made yourself a Botch, haven't you?'

Tesla's grin widened and the beading above her eye glowed brighter. She lifted her pointed chin so that he could see the makeup applied to the left side of her neck. "Too much?"

"Just enough," Lynx said, admiring how the makeup resembled pulsing wires that followed the line of tendons in her neck. His voice took on a kidding tone. "How long did it take you to make those clothes look like they've been worn for years?"

"Well, I had to do quite a job on them ..." She looked at him with slitted eyes. "Are you teasing me?"

"You bet, it's part of the package," he said. "You know, with that fancy get-up and expert makeup, we're going to have to think of a new name for you. A Botch name."

Tesla considered this as she walked around the fountain, once again toying with her braid. "You all have such unusual names," she began.

"They're from the books we still have, creatures whose pictures we see there. Like mine, Lynx is a big strong cat." His jaw jutted as he boasted. "And then there's Wren, Slug's mom. The way she talks and flits around our pod, if you'd see her you'd think she was just like a little bird. And Phlox ..."

"Phlox, that's a funny kind of name." Tesla had stopped her circumnavigation of the fountain and stared at him through the stream of water falling from the stone fish in the middle. Lynx felt defensiveness surge through him and tamped it down.

"Phlox is my baby sister, and she's named after a flower. It suits her," he said shortly.

"I'm sorry," she said, pulling her tapered fingertips through the end of her braid, avoiding his gaze.

Lynx softened. "It's all right. So what about you? What do you want to be called?"

Tesla started circling the fountain again, passing in front of him and tickling him under the chin with the end of her braid before continuing. She looked up, through the woven green vines and beyond, to the upper reaches of the Dome.

"I really love transporting, you know, how I go back up there? That feeling of weightlessness and the wind flowing over my skin and through my clothes and hair." She glanced at him and a faint pink touched her cheekbones. "Maybe a creature that flies?"

Lynx circled the fountain in the opposite direction, tugging on her other braid as he passed by her. "Well," he began, remembering back to earlier days when he sat perched on one of Wren's knees, Slug on the other, Phlox nestled in the middle. "There were birds before the climate changed, you could be a kind of bird, like an osprey or a tern or a swift. They are all pretty quick and graceful."

Tesla thought about this and shook her head.

"Oho, picky about your Botch identity, are you?"

Tesla colored again and Lynx made a mental note to tease her as much as he could.

"Okay then, how about a bat? Naw, too ugly. Maybe an insect like a dragonfly or a butterfly or … hey! I got it! What about a Luna moth? They were these large moths the size of my hands," he crossed his two hands, metal and skin, backs toward Tesla with fingers spread. "They were this beautiful green color but the really cool thing was that they had fake eyes on the bottom half of their wings, so that any creature out hunting would mistake the fake eyes for those of a much larger creature and leave them alone. Masters of disguise, not unlike you and your fancy make-up." He traced a forefinger, not touching but close enough, along her temple where the false wiring shimmered and pulsed.

She reached up and caught his hand, then let it go just as quickly. "Disguise and illusion. What I'm best at. I'll take it. You can call me Luna," she said.

"Okay Luna," he murmured, watching as the beading above her eye began to pulse, the color growing stronger. "How does that make-up work?" he asked. "Why does it change?"

"It …" she hesitated. "It speeds up with my heart rate." Her eyes pointed downwards, dark lashes splayed on her cheekbones. When she looked in his eyes, Lynx felt his own heart stop. *Luna, that's about perfect.* When he found his voice, he muttered hoarsely, "Let's get this show on the road."

Tesla, now Luna, nodded. Lynx didn't look back to see if she was following him out of the garden. He knew she was fluttering right behind him.

# CHAPTER NINE

On the way back to the bank of elevators, Lynx decided that he would first take Tesla to the outer Rim, especially since she'd told him she'd never been. He still couldn't imagine introducing her Botch self to his family so soon after his conversation with Wren about the A-One who had saved him.

"My sister, Lilly, goes out there all the time. She's the crazy one," Tesla filled him in as they made their way to the edge of the Dome. "Not like me. I'm the sensible one." Her mouth pulled downward as she said this, her eyebrows stitching together.

"Sure," Lynx said with a half-laugh. "Because saving a Botch and then making him take you Below is so very *sensible*."

She looked at him with a vulnerability he hadn't seen before, eyes wide and serious, and, as she realized he was teasing her again, she joined her laughter with his. "I guess you're right," she conceded.

"Wait 'til your sister gets a load of you," he added. They were at the perimeter, close to where Slug had been pulled off the wall and where Lynx had met Tesla for the first time. Lynx leapt up and caught the top of the wall with his metal hand, feet scrabbling until he could catch his footing. Once he was perched on top, he held out his human hand for Tesla. She slipped her cold sliver of a hand into his and he pulled her up. Gauging the distance down the other side, they glanced at each other and, hands joined, jumped.

The access port that he and LeftEye had used only that morning was still active. Normally, Lynx would've had to learn the new codes because the programmers changed them daily. *But,* Lynx thought in amazement, *it's still today. Back out we go.* He considered the idea that he was about to take an A-One with no landboat experience out into what could be a superstorm. Could he handle the boat by himself and also make sure that they both didn't get swept away? *Too late now,* he thought as he punched the numbers into the keyboard to the left of the pressurized doors.

The port opened and admitted them into an environment that was mercifully not as hostile as it had been hours before. It wasn't clear, but it wasn't storming yet either, Lynx noted with relief. He unhitched the locks on the landboat's cover while Tesla stood nearby. Once he'd removed it, he helped Tesla into the boat and settled her as he deployed the sails, glancing at the dim disk that he supposed was the sun.

*I guess we can glean some energy today. Every little bit helps.* He had to pull hard to raise the metallic sails, parallel layers of sun-absorbing fabric stretching twenty feet up to the top of the mast. When they were hoisted and began to glow a muted orange from the spare sunlight they were absorbing, he disengaged the anchors, each of them retracting with a snap that made Tesla jump. Lynx grinned at her to loosen her up. She smiled back, but just barely.

They started moving with a jerk, eliciting a gasp from Tesla, who grabbed the rail in alarm.

"Totally normal," Lynx shouted over the steady winds. *And this from the girl who can't get enough of transporting.* Then they were off, picking up speed in the barren landscape. The sun was still hidden by the sheer veil of gray gritty clouds. The outer ring of domes looked like a string of dirty pearls laid out in front of them. From Lynx's perch at the helm, ostensibly steering the boat but also watching Tesla out of the corner of his eye, he could see she was relaxing, and—wait! Was she smiling? She turned back to him, her braids whipping across her face and her eyes glowing.

*Atta girl,* Lynx thought, giving her a thumbs up.

She nodded and turned back to watch the domes of the outer Rim grow larger.

Thirty minutes later, they arrived. The sun had almost broken through the layer of yellow clouds scudding high above them. It looked as if they would have a rare moment of fair weather.

Tesla, or rather Luna, had seemed almost to enjoy the ride. Now she was moving about the boat, following Lynx's instructions to secure the cover to the sides.

*No one would believe me,* Lynx thought as he deployed two anchors, forward and aft. *An A-One listening to my commands. Surreal.* Of course he wouldn't mention anything to Tesla, especially now that she seemed to be having fun for the first time since they'd met. The boat secured, Lynx vaulted off onto the dusty floor of the desert. He reached up to help Tesla down, being extra careful not to hurt her as his large metal hand encircled her waist. As they strode toward the port, to Lynx's surprise Tesla didn't push his hand away but held it against the line of her waist as if it were totally natural.

Lynx did not usually visit this dome because it housed merely what helped the crops grow, not the crops themselves, and his missions took him to those domes that had what he needed to feed his family. Just visible through the thick glass was a shifting miasma of color. When the second set of doors slid open, Tesla gasped. Stretching out before them was a field of wildflowers. Other crops would be cultivated and maintained in straight lines, but not in this dome. Here everything grew wherever it could, creating a cacophony of color and movement. For this dome housed the bugs and bats that insured the other crops would keep growing; in here were the pollinators.

Flitting from flowers of every hue were thousands of butterflies.

The air was alive with the heady perfume of the blossoms and the drone of the bees going about their work. Tesla's face was pure wonder as she watched an overladen bumblebee buzz by, wings working madly to keep itself aloft under the burden of all that pollen.

"It's so ..." her voice died out as a purple and black butterfly flitted in front of her face, pausing as if to investigate her. "It's so beautiful. I never could've imagined anything like it."

Tesla moved away, dropping Lynx's hand from her waist, and stepped into the tall grass swaying from the breeze made by gigantic fans at the edge of the dome. She put her hands out to either side of her as she walked through the field, which stretched to a hill in the distance. Lynx followed a few paces behind her, watching her face as she took in the myriad colors and smells. She usually looked so imperious, her face beautiful but also untouchable. Now, as she swiveled to follow the flight of a darting hummingbird, her face was that of a child in the middle of a dream. The hummingbird paused in front of her just as the butterfly had. Tesla reached out with a pale finger, attempting to touch the tip of the bird's tiny beak, but it was gone before she came close. She giggled, her finger hanging in the humid air, and looked at Lynx with her gray-green eyes gone wide.

"Thank you for bringing me here."

Abashed, he ducked his head.

"What, what? Who's there now?" A strange voice from just ahead startled them both. Scanning the undulating tawny grasses, the rainbow of flowers, and the universe of small flying insects and birds made it hard for Lynx to pick out any particular movement that was out of place. Tesla had moved back by his side, both of her hands gripping his large metal forearm. Lynx nodded to her with more conviction than he felt.

"Hello?" Lynx asked.

This time, a small mound that Lynx had assumed was a pile of earth popped up from a patch of columbine. It was a sun-bleached hat with a fine sheen of sand cascading off of it. A man about sixty years old with a reddish moustache looked out from under the brim. He straightened up, revealing a tall body, and strode toward them. The instruments attached to his wide belt banged his thighs at every step.

"Hello there," he said. "Thought I heard voices." He approached with hand outstretched. Lynx pushed Tesla behind him and squared his shoulders to the stranger. He took the hand that was offered him; the man shook it until Lynx thought it would fall off.

"I say, mighty good to have company. What you come out for, a look around? Not a bad spot, what what?" The man's moustache jumped with enthusiasm above his thin lips.

"What?" Lynx asked.

"Exactly right there, what what?"

"Wait, what's what? I mean, what?" Lynx tried again.

"I say, are you having some trouble there, m'boy? Do you speak English?" The man enunciated each syllable. Lynx could feel Tesla shake with silent laughter against his back. A few awkward moments passed as the strangers regarded one another until a low-flying squadron of blue bottle flies buzzed between them.

"I say," the man said, twisting the end of his moustache.

"What do you say?" Lynx asked, still confused.

"Exactly right that. What what?" The man craned his sandy head around to get a good look at Tesla. "Not just you then? Who've you got behind you there?"

Tesla stepped forward, extending her own hand in welcome. Lynx grabbed her wrist, pulling her hand down out of fear the man would be successful in shaking it off. The man didn't seem to notice as he was busy pulling off his hat, sweeping it to one side, and giving Tesla a deep bow.

"Lady, I am honored by your presence. Mendel at your service, head apiarist and man about town." He looked up at her and waggled his eyebrows, which resembled blond caterpillars.

Tesla glanced at Lynx, who shrugged. "Please," she said. "Please get up. I'm Tes … I'm Luna. I'm very pleased to meet you."

The man straightened up, replacing the hat on the tousle of reddish curls it had concealed. "So you're an Underdweller then? Yes, I can see your modifications. Luna? Interesting name, what what?"

"What!" Lynx said with exasperation. Tesla swatted him on the shoulder.

"Yes, I was named for a Luna moth. Do you know what that is?"

"Do I know what? Mi'lady please!" the man sputtered. "Not only do I know what one is, I have a cave full of them. Would you like to see them? Perhaps a spot of tea to tempt you as well? We have the freshest honey out here on the Rim, as you might've guessed." He waved his hands at the buzzing atmosphere. Without waiting for an answer he turned and strode off, leaving a swath of flattened grass in his wake. Tesla grabbed Lynx's hand and tugged, following the man with a mischievous grin on her face. "Are you sure about this?" Lynx whispered at her back. "What if he finds out who you are?"

Tesla spun, walking backwards, one eyebrow arched. "Now Lynx, you're the one who said I should get out more. I'm just following your advice!" She followed Mendel's retreating back.

"Did I really say that? I don't remember saying that, *Luna*," he said, emphasizing her name.

As they walked, Mendel rattled off the Latin names of the flowers they were passing as well as their medicinal properties. "This is Asclepias tuberosa, butterfly weed. Great for coughs and the like, what?" He stopped to finger one of the bright orange blossoms, startling a dragonfly perched on its tip. "Ow," he cried out, slapping at his forearm. "Shame that," he said, plucking off a bee and studying the wound. "He's a goner, lost his stinger in me arm. Ah well, no use wasting the protein." To the horror of Lynx and Tesla, Mendel popped the bee into his mouth and chewed. "Not so bad, really. Faintly sweet. Off we go!"

"I think I'm going to pass on tea," Lynx whispered to Tesla's back, making her giggle.

On the other side of the small rise, the hillside turned from long grasses to rocky outcropping. Halfway down the steep slope stood a ramshackle wooden house and almost equal to it in length and girth was an attached glass greenhouse, windows covered with condensation from the heat trapped within it.

"Home," remarked Mendel.

They threaded their way around the structure and entered the greenhouse through a creaky glass door. The space, with shelving up to the rafters and skylights cracked to let out the heat, was filled with plants that all had glossy dark green leaves and long stems that drooped with the weight of the many blossoms weighing them down. The blooms looked like faces, but that was where the similarity between them ended. Each one was a combination of the most unlikely and exquisite colors. There were orange tiger stripes, pink polka dots, and white with the faintest blush of blue, to name a few. Passing through the crowded, muggy space, Lynx couldn't smell any fragrance from the flowers.

Mendel was watching his guests closely. "They don't have any fragrance, these Orchidaceae. I made them that way."

Tesla lifted her head from where she was studying a bright red bloom that faded to a sunny yellow in the middle. "Did you say you made them?"

"What, what? Well, of course, my dear. I made all of them. And since I made them, there is no need for them to reproduce. I'm already lacking the space, you see." He put his finger under a bloom, chucking it under its chin as you would a small child, which set the stem atremble. "I've tried other creations, but they haven't quite made it. Let me show you." He led them to the back of the greenhouse which opened into the house proper. It was a claustrophobic space, crowded with mismatched chairs and a wooden table that overflowed with papers and instruments.

"Back in a flash," Mendel said and disappeared into a kitchen to the right. Lynx and Tesla stood in the middle of the room in amazement. On the walls were animals, stuffed and unmoving, and these were like none Lynx had ever seen in books or otherwise. Tesla slipped her hand into his and gripped it. They were like animals out of a dream, or a nightmare. A gigantic bat with a yellow tabby cat's head was mounted on a wooden baseboard. An otter with a fish body looked down with disapproval from its permanent perch atop a log. A lizard with a parrot's head and vibrantly colored wings sat unmoving in a glass case. Most grotesque of all was the long snake frozen mid-climb on the side of a bookcase, its head that of an enlarged praying mantis. Lynx tried to concentrate on the outlandish creatures before him, but he could only center his attention on the cool hand locked in his.

Behind them, Mendel stumbled into the room, two mugs of steaming liquid clutched in one fist, a mason jar of golden honey and a spoon gripped in the other. He made his way to the cluttered table and, shoving papers out of the way with his elbow, he plunked the mugs down with a clatter.

"Ah, you've met my pets. Tea?"

Lynx ignored the offer. "Pets?"

"Yes, well, what I was saying before. The orchids seem to be the only creatures I have a hand at manipulating. The others have all failed in some crucial way. Here's Calliope," he gestured to the lizard. "And Thalia." That was the otter. "Clio." He scratched the unmoving cat/bat under its chin. "And my darling, Pandora." Mendel ran his finger lovingly down the spine of the great snake. Beside him, Lynx could feel Tesla shudder. "Anyone for tea?"

Both Lynx and Tesla shook their heads simultaneously and emphatically.

"Well then," Mendel said with regret, staring down at his hands for a moment. "You know what? I have this strange feeling that I used to be quite good at making things like this." He gazed into the blind eyes of the mantis. "It's like it's on the tip of my tongue, knowing how, but then it just slips away." He spread his palms out in front of him. Moments passed while Mendel stood in the middle of his congested living room, looking like the human version of one of his immobile creations. Tesla disengaged her hand from Lynx's, tiptoeing over to Mendel and touching his elbow. He startled, and she jumped back. "Right, yes my dear?"

"The moths, Mr. Mendel. Weren't you going to show us the luna moths?"

"Quite right. I say, dear girl, you are quite exquisite. And oddly familiar." Mendel reached out to touch Tesla's face but she leaned far back, pushing into Lynx's chest. Mendel snapped his hand down. "Right, the moths. Walk this way, if you don't mind." With that he spun on his foot and strode through the door in the back of the room. Above it was an unusual symbol, writ in red. It was a square bisected into four equal quadrants. Each of the four squares that made up the larger one had two letters next to it, with either an uppercase or a lowercase "A."

As they approached, Lynx saw that it wasn't actually pitch black beyond the doorway. There was a faint green glow. He followed Tesla and Mendel into a darkness that smelled like a cave: moldy and earthy at once. It was at least ten degrees cooler than the room where they'd been. Lynx stumbled, and as he was steadying himself on the slick surface of a rock wall, a scuttling shape scurried across his hand and made him leap forward with an inward shriek. He could just make out the two figures in front of him, outlined with green light that emanated from the cavern ahead.

"Come on then," Mendel's voice echoed in the wide passage. Tesla and Lynx stumbled after Mendel, who had no trouble at all with the uneven ground. After a few minutes of fumbling down a slight slope, they entered a much larger cavern. The same green glow emanated from mushrooms punctuating the walls, which stretched up a good forty feet, and from hundreds of glowing worms suspended from the ceiling by gossamer filaments. The air was also filled with the blinking of thousands of fireflies, or, as Mendel soon corrected them: lampyridae. Tesla reached up to touch a glowworm, but Mendel stopped her hand with his own.

"I'm afraid you won't want to do that, love," he said, his serious expression lit up by the insects' emanations. "The poison on them is for their prey, but it'll give you a nasty sting nonetheless." Sure enough, the filaments were beaded with tiny droplets reflecting light.

"What are they?" she asked.

"Glowworms, love. Lampyris noctiluca and arachnocampa. Mighty helpful little buggers. But that wasn't what we came for, we wanted to meet your namesake. Careful not to disturb the bats." Mendel pointed up. Lynx, following the man's gesture, could just make out the dimpled surface of the ceiling and what he imagined were the huddled bodies of thousands of bats.

"Now where could they ... aha!" Mendel took two long steps toward where several luna moths were ranged sleepily along the far wall. He slid his hand under the nearest and largest one; its wingspan eclipsed the man's palm. "Here she is, actia luna." He walked over to Tesla. who stood gazing up at the hundreds of glowing worms dangling from the ceiling like a living chandelier. "She's a beaut."

Mendel deposited the luna moth, shimmering moss green with large false eyes on its wings, onto Tesla's shoulder. It flapped in protest and then settled, its wide wings almost touching her face as it fluttered. Tesla was frozen. She looked at Lynx with eyes the same shade of green as the moth.

"Quite right," Lynx said, still staring at her. "One of the most beautiful things I've ever seen."

# CHAPTER TEN

I t had taken Tesla a moment to get used to the blinding daylight after they'd found their way outside the dome. Mendel had offered them tea again but they'd both refused, for as interesting as the man was, his exhaustive knowledge of plants, bugs, and bats had worn thin. Before they'd parted ways, Lynx had promised to bring a special delivery to Mendel on his next journey to the outer Rim.

"I'd like a pet," Mendel had said. "Not something that will eat up all these creatures, but something that would be company, what what? I'm not sure I can take another one of my own creations failing."

"Right," Lynx had agreed, winking at Tesla. "I'm sure we can think of something." With that they'd started off down the hill toward the port at the other side of the meadow.

"Wait!" They'd turned back to Mendel as he'd flourished a flower in his hand, bowing to Tesla once again. "For you, dear Luna. A token of beauty for bringing light back into an old man's eyes."

Tesla had taken the conical bloom, violet outside and bright yellow inside, and had tucked it beneath her cap and behind her ear. She'd squeezed Mendel's hand. "Thank you."

Outside, the wind still hadn't picked up. As they weighed anchor and hoisted the sails, Lynx kept up a running commentary about the weather. "As fine as it is, I can't help but worry that this great stretch of weather might be the harbinger of some very nasty storms to come."

Tesla looked up at the cirrus clouds making a quick path above them.

"Some of the largest super-tornadoes came directly after the nicest weather anyone had ever seen." As he spoke, Tesla saw Lynx flip a switch next to the steering column. In response to her questioning glance, he said, "Magnets in the keel."

Tesla felt the boat settle into its carriage, shifting forwards and backwards on its rugged wheels.

"Where are we off to now?" Tesla asked him, grabbing the main sheet and hoping he would say Below.

Lynx fidgeted at the helm, not meeting her eyes.

"Water dome," he stated, yanking the tiller to port and releasing the catch as the boat began to pull away.

"I know what you're doing, Lynx," Tesla said.

He adjusted ropes and lines as Tesla studied him. "I don't know what you're talking about, Tes."

"Yes you do, and it won't work."

"What won't work?"

She flicked the end of the main sheet in his direction. "You still have to take me Below. You promised, and you said Underdwell ... I mean Botches always keep their word. Always." With that Tesla turned towards the bow of the boat, watching the string of lesser domes dotting the landscape off their starboard side.

When they entered the water dome half an hour later, Tesla realized there was no land in this dome at all. The minute she walked onto a corrugated metal platform, all she could hear and smell was water. The cobalt blue of a deep lake stretched as far as she could see. Wires were strung across it at many different angles, and large platforms were erected on poles at various intervals like gigantic osprey nests. As they climbed towards the nearest one fifty feet above them, Lynx told her that the basin of the dome had been dug several hundred feet deep, good for storing massive amounts of fresh water as well as accessing the remaining aquifer with limited drilling.

Lynx held out a harness to Tesla, who took it and strapped it around her lithe body, then stood with arms raised and eyes closed as he moved around her, pulling the straps taut over her body and securing the buckles.

"There," he said, giving the last strap a jerk.

"Now what?" Tesla said, her eyes on his.

He showed her the link on the back of his harness. "We clip these to this." His metal hand grabbed a wire that was attached to the framework above their heads. He took her link, snapping it to the wire with a clink. He then attached them together with a spare rope as a precaution.

The whole metal structure swayed in the wind fifty heart-wrenching feet in the air. The wire made a sharp downward angle to the first platform, half a mile away. Tesla gave Lynx a curt nod and leapt off the platform, arms spread wide in a swan dive. Soon she was whizzing the length of the wire, hair streaming straight out behind her like a banner. The fear that gripped her stomach soon subsided, turning into pure elation. *This is so much better than transporting! It's like flying!*

Although the platform had seemed to be a mere punctuation mark from where they'd started, it approached at breakneck speed. As they zoomed nearer, Tesla could feel her forward motion slowed by the rope linking her with Lynx. She turned awkwardly to look back and saw that he had his metal hand out, palm facing the metal tower. *I bet he's got magnets in there,* she thought. They slowed almost to a stop and Lynx wound his hand around her swinging body to steady them both.

Tesla grabbed onto the railing of a spiral staircase, pulling herself over the side and skipping down the stairs to the broad swath of woven netting. She extracted a small piece of fabric from a pocket under her broad belt. When Lynx reached her, she was unfolding a blanket, holding on to the corners of the yellow fabric and flapping it hard in the breeze. Every time she snapped the fabric, it grew in dimension, until it was large enough to accommodate two people.

"Grab that," she said. He grabbed two ends of the fluttering blanket and knelt, bringing it down. "I've brought you a surprise. Is there any way you can get some of that water?"

Lynx nodded, opening up his metal forearm and pulling out a neoprene bag. He closed the compartment and then, unlatching his hand still holding the canteen, he pushed it through the netting, pressing on a button until his hand dropped in a controlled fall down to the water. In a few moments he reeled both hand and canteen back up.

Meanwhile, Tesla laid various items onto the blanket, hoping that Lynx would be impressed with what she'd brought for him. There were tiny pieces of food, resembling a set in a doll's house. There were even napkins the size of pencil erasers. Taking the canteen out of Lynx's hands, Tesla poured some water into her palm and used her fingertips to sprinkle the miniature picnic.

"Watch out," she said, and just in time. With a noise halfway between a "sproing" and a "pop," the items between the two teenagers expanded. In a split second, there appeared a platter of sandwiches; cherries, so oversized that there were only two; and the napkins, fluttering in the cool breeze.

"Wow," Lynx said. "Just wow."

"Totally cool, right, what what?" Tesla agreed with a grin, lifting each sandwich and inspecting its interior.

Lynx crooked an eyebrow at her. "Double wow. Was that a joke, Miss Tes? Wonders never cease."

She stuck her tongue out at him and tossed a silvery braid over her shoulder. "We have: cheese and pickle sandwiches. Ick. Oh, here's hummus with some tomatoes." She pulled the bread off one side of a sandwich to show him the brown spread and the tiny tomatoes sprinkled across the surface.

"Umm, cheese and pickle sounds … okay."

"You're braver than I am." Tesla handed Lynx the sandwich of thick brown bread. With only a little hesitation, he took a bite. "Thish ish really good," he said through a mouthful. "The picklesh are shweet with the cheeshe."

"Thrilled, really," Tesla said, nibbling a corner of her sandwich after drawing the napkin across her lap.

They ate in silence for many minutes, the lapping of the water mixing with the odd hum of the wind blowing through the criss-crossing wires. When they'd finished, Lynx handed Tesla the remnants of his sandwich, which she tucked into a sack the same color and material as the blanket they were sitting on. She folded it onto itself and it became half its regular size, then half of that, then half of that, until it was the size of a matchbook, which she tucked back into her pocket. When she looked up, she found Lynx staring at her. "What?" she asked.

"That bag, this blanket, should I even ask how?"

"It's ergodic theory, in its most basic form. But really, when you think about it, it's no more amazing than that arm of yours, is it?"

Lynx flexed his metal fist. "I guess not."

She tossed a cherry the size of a softball at him and he caught it without puncturing its fragile skin.

"Like that," she said. "How can it be so strong and yet so gentle at the same time?"

"Practice, I guess. I mean, I was pretty haphazard with it when Chick first modified me, knocking things over and breaking stuff all the time. But I had to learn to be gentle, mainly because my sister was so little and her condition … I didn't want to hurt her."

"Phlox," Tesla supplied, rolling her cherry between her palms.

"Yes, that's right, Phlox. She's … delicate. She's had to have a lot of modifications. It's hard for her."

Tesla looked away from him then, a line forming between her brows. She couldn't quite put her feelings into words; yet it felt as if she'd forgotten something … something important, and was on the verge of remembering it.

"Hey," Lynx said. "What'd I say? It's not your fault she's the way she is. It's the darned plague."

Tesla looked back at him, trying hard to tamp down the miasma of emotions that were bubbling up. She felt like a pond in winter that wasn't fully frozen, liquid leaking around the edges. "Maybe it isn't my fault personally, but I'm an A-One, Lynx. I'm not Luna, I'm barely even Tesla, I'm X3721. I was just thinking that A-Ones need to *do* something about that plague."

Her statement hung in the air. Lynx looked mystified by her sudden change of mood. She attempted a smile. "I guess what makes me different is that I don't accept things as they are. If I disagree with something then I want to change it. Which is why I want to go Below, to see for myself that what they say about Botches not having feelings or loyalty or love is wrong, all wrong. That way, I can make a case to Skinner, with proof."

"Skinner?"

"Skinner is my male producer. My father, I guess." The word left an acrid taste in her mouth.

"You call him your producer, that's weird."

"I guess it depends what you're used to. I've never known anything different. When I saw you protect your brother, I knew what I'd been taught was wrong. That's why I want you to take me there, so that I can see for myself what's really true and what isn't, not just what someone tells me to believe." She looked at the fruit she'd been rolling between her palms. The skin had ruptured, oozing blood-red juice onto her hands.

"All right," Lynx conceded after a few moments. "I'll do it."

She shook her head. "What?"

"What, what?" He replied with a grin. "I said I'll do it, Tesla, I'll take you down to meet my family. I was having a hard time with it but now it seems …" He trailed off. "And maybe when you see the effects of the plague, you'll tell the programmers Above," he said.

"And maybe they can help find a cure, once I show them that Botches are just like A-Ones."

They began to move toward one another, and Tesla knew that this was the moment in which she would leave all else behind her. His lips were cold at first, but soon warmed to the intensity of their kiss. The lake-tangy breeze, the whine of the wires overhead, the lilt and splash of the waves beneath them faded away and all that was left was him: Lynx.

When they broke apart, Tesla felt embarrassed to meet his eyes until he said softly, "Hey," and then again "Hey." She gave him a quirky little smile. He wrapped his arm around her waist and pulled her across the blanket to settle in the crook of his arm. She relaxed into his side.

All of sudden she stiffened and sat up straighter. "Oh!" Tesla said, her mouth gaping. She had never seen anything like it. Across the broad stretch of water and through the skin of this lesser dome, the sun was setting. The weather had remained clear and now the rays of light struck the transparent side with an array of fiery oranges, purples, and reds. The rainbow of light licked each wavelet with a different color. The effect was that of a moving, dancing tapestry of water and light. *It's incredible that such a beautiful landscape could be so hostile,* she thought.

"Oh," she said again, leaning back into Lynx's arm to enjoy the fireworks of the sunset. The high-tech makeup pulsed with her delighted heartbeat, as she wondered if they would really be able to destroy the plague.

# CHAPTER ELEVEN

T esla and Lynx whizzed across the darkening landscape away
from the shrinking ring of lesser domes. Lynx held fast to the
tiller as they barrelled toward the bright lights of the city Dome.
From this angle, and in this surprising stretch of clear weather, it
looked like a giant tree teeming with lights. The base of the Dome
only showed the long wall that ringed the inner side of it. Rising
above that were the shapes of the Middlespacers' dwellings, all
crannies and turrets, jutting out at odd angles and tunneling deep
into the trunk. Far above it all, even above the band of commercial
shops and clubs, unwound the long branches of the A-Ones.

"Which one is yours? Can you tell from out here?" He had
to holler into the head wind to be heard. Tesla was holding on to
the flower Mendel had given her to prevent it from flying into the
atmosphere. Her face paint glowed, highlighting her features in the
darkening twilight. She looked up at the curving massiveness that
was the Dome. Lynx wondered if she couldn't see which one was
hers or didn't want to tell him.

"The top one," she said simply. Lynx craned his neck and could
just make out an ivory disc crowning the spread of branches.

"The one with the blue lights?"

"Yes."

Lynx's low whistle was lost in the wind. *Why would she*

*be embarrassed about it?* He wondered. Then it struck him. *Not wanting to introduce her to my family is like I'm embarrassed by her, or embarrassed by my family. I wonder which it is.* He sat uncomfortably with this idea for the time it took to reach the access port on the outskirts of the Dome. *Maybe a little of both,* he decided. *No more of that, I'll take her down and see what she comes up with as a cover story. She's a big girl, X3721, for Dome's sake. She can take care of it on her own.*

The decision, even if it was the decision to say nothing at all, filled him with resolve. He hurled the tiller over to the far side and the landboat drifted in a semi-circle. Bounding toward the mast, Lynx untied the mainsail's halyard as the boat pivoted until it was parallel to the port. It stopped as the magnets in the keel and the metals in the ground drew together and halted the boat's forward motion.

Tesla did not seem as nervous as she had been on her maiden voyage. She coiled the main sheet, looping the bundle over the end of the tiller before springing off the boat and landing with a thud onto the dirt. Lynx deployed the anchors and locked the cover's hasps before leaping down to join her. The vacuum inside the port was deafening after the noisome wind outside. Tesla was deep in thought, playing with the end of her braid as they made their way toward the bank of elevators beyond the bazaar. It was early evening. Tesla watched some departing A-Ones transporting to their domiciles and Lynx wondered if she wanted to go with them. Catching his curious gaze, Tesla smiled, one eyebrow cocked.

"How long does it take?" she asked, gesturing toward the elevators.

"To get Below?" Lynx was twisting the ring at the top, nudging the giant metal doors open a crack. "I guess it depends on how far down we go." He forced his metal hand into the slit and wrenched the door the rest of the way open, holding it as Tesla climbed onto the roof of the elevator. He pulled the wire that closed the doors, securing them in total darkness. The only light came from Tesla's face. He grabbed the cable and stepped closer to her, watching as the gems above her eyes started to pulse more rapidly.

"Tesla," he slipped his human hand around her waist, following the loop of her leather belt. Her arms slid up around his neck as she brought her face closer to his. "Are you sure you want to do this? You don't have to, not to prove anything to me. I think you're as brave as it gets anyways."

She cocked her head. By the light of her makeup, Lynx could see she was staring at his lips. "I've never wanted to do anything more in my entire life," she said, sending chills down his spine as she brushed his lips with hers. It felt like the kiss of a butterfly's wing. "And I'm not doing it for you. I'm doing it for me." She stared into his eyes this time, perhaps to see if he believed her, and kissed him again. Their first kiss had been tentative, two strange mouths exploring each other's new dimensions. This kiss, however, was as if he was right at the heart of her. He felt that somehow, instead of a girl, he held a living, beating, burning soul in his arms. When their lips parted, they stayed together, forehead to forehead, breathing hard. She laid a cool hand against his cheek.

"That decides it." Lynx knelt, flipping open the compartment on his arm and lighting up the small torch in his finger. "We're going Below."

The disembodied voice drifted through the metal at their feet. "Floor please? At the moment ..."

"Sub 33," Lynx shouted, staring up into Tesla's eager grin. He stood and wrapped an arm around her again. His large metal fingers grasped the cables above them. "Hang on, this is quite a ride."

Lynx felt confident all the way home until he stepped into the hallway of his pod with Tesla just behind him. They hadn't discussed a plan, yet here they were, facing the door that Lynx had been coming in and out of for the last seven years. It felt so strange to him that it was hard to believe it was the same one. *Or maybe it's me who's changed.* He shot one glance at Tesla and then he pushed the door open to whatever lay in wait for them on the other side.

They paused in the hallway. Tesla's eyes were on him as he listened. He could hear Slug in the front room, and Phlox's laughter. And then a voice he couldn't quite place but which was very familiar. But no Wren and no Chick, which for the moment was just fine. He strode down the hallway, pushing aside the flowered curtain. Phlox and Slug were seated with their backs to the window. Phlox was swaddled in a patchwork quilt, listening as Sage told them an animated story, all elbows and orange hair.

"He said that they all have showers that will turn the bubbles purple or whatever color they want, and that they can program them so that they'd be showering on an ice cap!"

"Come on, Sage, you don't believe everything you hear from the Middlespacers." Slug remarked.

"Why would they need to lie? They don't, not about A-Ones," Sage countered.

Tesla cringed behind his back. Lynx decided that this was their moment. "Ahem."

"Lynx!" Phlox said, her face alight. "Hey there big fella," Sage began, giving him a bear hug. "Where in Dome … oh!" She dropped her arms, peering around him at Tesla. With a flip of a braid, Tesla stepped around him, legs akimbo.

"Hi," she said, her makeup pulsing wildly. It was her only sign of nervousness. "I'm Luna."

A stunned silence filled the front room until Sage broke it.

"Sage," she said, sticking out a skinny hand in greeting.

Tesla smiled with relief as she shook Sage's hand, her makeup's wild vibrations ebbing. Slug rose from his spot next to Phlox and swung over to where Tesla stood.

"Nice to meetcha," he said, with only one questioning glance thrown toward Lynx. Tesla fistbumped Slug's outstretched hand and walked over to where Phlox was staring up at her from a nest of quilts.

"And you must be Phlox," Tesla said. She held out her hand and, after a moment's hesitation, Phlox slid her hand out from under the covers. As she shook it, Tesla did not seem put off by the fact that it was entirely made of metal. She held it for a moment longer, cocking her head at Phlox. "You know, it's so funny, you look a lot like my sister. I mean A LOT like her."

A prickling sensation rippled up Lynx's back.

Phlox snaked her hand back under the covers, giving Tesla a wide smile. "What's her name?"

"Lilly," Tesla responded. "She has blonde hair, like me, and your coloring is very different, but her face and your face ... you could be twins!"

"I don't think that we could be twins," Phlox said, pulling the quilt up more snugly around her chin. "Does she have a lot of modifications? Is she made of metal, like me? It's 'cuz of the plague. Wren says it has a thing for me."

Tesla looked down at her hands. "No. No I guess she doesn't. She doesn't have any at all." Tesla was thoughtful for a moment, her makeup's vibrations once again speeding up as she considered something. "This plague is horrible! Something has to be done about it." Changing the subject, she leaned toward Phlox. "So, I've heard a lot about you from your brother."

"I haven't heard anything about you, Luna," Phlox said. "Where are you from?"

Lynx clenched his fist, reminding himself that he wasn't going to intercede, that Tesla could do this on her own.

"I'm from another dome."

Sage and Slug sat down next to Phlox. "What do you mean there's another dome?" Sage said.

"There is, far far away. It tooks us weeks to get here."

"I didn't think Botches could travel that freely," Slug said.

"They can't, normally." Tesla's speech came more naturally the deeper she dug. "But we have family here, and things weren't working out in the other dome. So we stowed away on a caravan of land yachts," she glanced at Lynx who nodded once, "big ones, ones that are meant to travel large distances. It's just me and my sister now."

"Like us, Lynx," said Phlox, looking at her older brother. "Like when we arrived here and Wren took us in."

"Talking about me again?" came Wren's voice from behind them. Lynx jumped and faced her as Wren came through the curtain laden with cloth bags. "Lynx, give a hand, would you?"

He complied, taking three of the heaviest-looking bags from her as she assessed the scene. "Is this your *friend* that you helped out today?" She nudged him with a sharp elbow.

"Yes," Lynx said, dropping the bags on the table. "Luna, this is Wren. Wren, Luna."

Wren strode over to where Tesla stood next to the windows and shook her outstretched hand. "Pleased to meet you."

"Same here," Tesla said.

"It's funny," Wren returned to where Lynx had spread out the different items. "I think I know everyone Below, but I've never seen you before."

"She was just telling us that she and her sister caught a ride on a caravan to find their family," Phlox said excitedly. She had high color in her cheeks as she looked up at Tesla. "Just like Lynx and me, Wren. And Luna says I look just like her sister. Not the hair but our faces, she said we could be twins!"

"Really?" Wren asked, winding a bolt of fabric in her hands. "Then her sister must be very beautiful." Wren smiled at Phlox but a wariness crept into her eyes.

Lynx's uneasiness grew, like a unwanted cough. He tried his best to keep breathing smoothly but that tickle kept returning. *When did it start? Oh yeah, when she said that thing about Phlox and her sister.* He grabbed the cloth from Wren's hands. "Where's Chick?"

"He went out to the grid. He'll be back later. Can I get you all something to eat?"

"Thank you but we just ate," Tesla said.

"Right, tea then?"

"That'd be … that'd be great."

Wren moved to the small kitchen, stowing the items she carried in her arms as she went. Tesla moved to her side. "Can I help, please? I hate to be idle."

Wren handed her a tin of stacked biscuits and a jar of tea. "A plate for the biscuits is overhead. Slug and Lynx, can you two please stash the rest of this in the back storage unit?"

When Lynx returned to the front room, Wren had set Phlox up at the table. Tesla carried a steaming teapot and a plate of biscuits to the table, chatting with Sage. One glance at Wren, and Lynx could tell that something wasn't right. It matched the bolus of dread in his own throat. She was behind Phlox and her usual well-tempered features were dark and her knuckles white where they gripped the back of the chair. She looked up at him with burning eyes, jerking her head toward the back hallway and stalking out of the room. Lynx found her there, metal fingertips tattooing a rhythm on the wall.

"She's one of them, isn't she?" Wren growled. "She's an A-One."

Lynx coughed. He considered playing it dumb for a split second, but one look at her glowering visage was enough to convince him that it wasn't a great idea. "Yes," he said with defeat.

"For Dome's sake! I told you not to mess with her any more than you had to! And what did you do? You brought her here! How could you be so incredibly stupid?" Wren was breathing fast.

"Wren, I'm … sorry. I didn't realize …" Lynx felt like something had broken off inside of him, something sharp that was jabbing just under his ribs. Wren had never spoken to him like this before. He'd never even heard her raise her voice.

"And now she's in there, with Phlox, making her laugh, making Phlox like her, when in the end she'll do just what they all do." Wren glanced down the hallway; Lynx turned, holding his metal arm across his churning stomach. In the doorway stood Tesla, her light hair glowing in the darkness of the hall.

"In the end I'll do what?" she asked, her voice ringing across the small space.

"You'll leave. Your kind always does, with broken things in your wake," Wren spat at her. "And that's exactly what I want you to do right now. Leave!"

Phlox's high-pitched voice filtered through the curtain. "We can hear everything you're saying, guys. You might as well come in here."

Wren threw a searing glare Lynx's way and stalked down the hall, past Tesla, whipping the curtain aside as she went. Lynx followed but paused by Tesla's side and squeezed her elbow. "C'mon, maybe we can talk some sense into her."

They entered the front room, where Wren once again stood behind Phlox's chair.

Lynx wrapped an arm around Tesla's waist. "Wren," he started, still wary of his foster mother's wrath. "Wren, she's a good person. She's not like the others. I know it."

Wren laughed, a hoarse growl of a chuckle. "And how would you know that? You've been acquainted all of what, two days? If that?"

"It's enough," Lynx's chin jutted into the air. "She saved me, Wren, she saved my life, doesn't that count for anything?"

"And how much did it cost her, saving your life?" Wren was

speaking to Lynx but her eyes were on Tesla. "How much did she have to risk to rescue you from that Evolutionist?"

Lynx paused and looked into Tesla's face. "She just told him to let me go."

"And he did. Did she even have to raise her voice?"

Again, Lynx took a moment to consider. "No," he said quietly.

Tesla stepped forward. "I want to explain something. I didn't come here to make trouble, but they teach us things up there, things about the Botches that aren't true. They tell us that you all have no feelings, no family, no friends. They tell us that you are barely human."

Lynx stiffened. He had known this all his life but to hear her say it was something else entirely. *Barely human, huh?*

"I now know that's not true. Everything I've learned about the Botches is a lie," Tesla continued. "I could see for myself the moment Lynx stood up for his brother at the bazaar. But most of us don't know that. They keep us tightly under wraps until we are launched at eighteen, and by that time we're too brainwashed to care."

Phlox spoke up. "Why would they go to the trouble of teaching you that? Why would it matter so much to them what you thought of us?"

Tesla fixed Phlox with a level stare, and when she spoke, her voice was gentle. "I don't know for sure, but I'm starting to put the pieces together."

*So am I,* Lynx thought.

Wren's rage broke through. "That's enough! I could care less what you think. We're doing fine on our own down here. You may think that we have no feelings, that we're not human," miniscule droplets of spit flew from Wren's lips. "But we do love, and we do have loyalty, more than you! Your lot just takes and takes without a thought to anyone else. Who's heartless then?"

A sudden silence descended on the group. Sage and Slug squirmed uncomfortably while Phlox looked around, eyes wide and mouth agape.

"This is my home. You're not up there in your crystal towers anymore. You're Below, and here, what *I* say goes. And right now I am telling you to get out. Get out and leave my son alone! You can't have him too!"

"All right," Tesla said as she cast a final pleading glance at Lynx, then turned and left the room.

Lynx walked over to where Wren stood, her hand covering her face. He touched her shoulder.

"I'm sorry," he said. "I'm so sorry that I brought her here. I didn't know it was going to upset you this much."

"You didn't know, and now you do." Wren's eyes burned into his. "You've got to cut her loose, Lynx. I can see by that gobsmacked look on your face that you're gaga about her. You've got to shake free from her spell, boy, or she'll only bring you trouble. I know ..." She trailed off, her glance shifting to Slug, who was still comforting Phlox. "There is one thing though. You've got to return her to Middlespace. She doesn't know her way back and she can't stay here. If other Botches find out, there could be a riot."

Lynx nodded. He strode out of the room after Tesla without saying a word.

Tesla was standing in the hallway outside their pod with her back to the door. She whirled at the sound of his footsteps.

He stopped, unable to keep his swirling emotions still enough to know how he was feeling. "Follow me, I've got to get you out of here."

"I'm ... I'm sorry," Tesla stuttered, bringing her hands up to his wrist. He shook them off briefly, then gave her a wan smile. Underneath his confused reaction to Wren's outburst was that piercing sensation. It felt as if he were desperately trying to stay

asleep but one long needle of light was constantly trained on his
eyelid. He stalked off down the hallway, hanging a left at the alley's
entrance, his long strides making Tesla skip-hop every few steps.
Right now, he wanted to get her up to her jeweled heights as fast
as possible, and then to try and forget an A-One called Tesla ever
existed.

"We've got to change all this," Tesla said from behind him. "We
can make this right."

"Yeah sure," Lynx scoffed. They'd arrived at the bank of
elevators. He pulled her up to the top of the second one, working
as fast as he could to get the thing moving surface-side.

"We have to talk to Skinner, you and me. Once he sees what
you're like, that you're not some kind of low-class robot, then we
can get him on our side." She bit her lip. Lynx cringed. He hated
her comment but also despised himself for noticing how cute her
gesture was.

"*Our* side?" Lynx said bitterly. "There is no *our* side, X3721. I'm
a Botch and you're an A-One. That's it."

He held onto Tesla stiffly, not looking at her as they began their
ascent.

"Lynx, look, I have an idea. Please hear me out. What would
make my case with Skinner even stronger was if I had proof. Real
living *Botch* proof." She let that sink in as they glided upward in
darkness, the disembodied voice from below counting off the
floors as they went. "Just consider it, if you came with me," she
tried again. "Then they couldn't present Botches as some sort
of mindless drones. They would have to understand that you're
human beings."

"And what could they do for us, Tes? Has your genetically
perfected brain figured it all out yet? Do you really know what
you're getting us into?"

"I don't, not fully. But I know that if Skinner meets you, and we tell him about the plague, he'll be able to find a cure. I know it. It could save Phlox."

The elevator stopped with a jerk. Lynx let go of Tesla as quickly as he could, tugging on the wires that opened the doors above them. He leapt out, not turning to see if she could manage it, and stood looking down the alleyway at the bazaar still teeming with Middlespacers. When she came abreast of him, he said, "Okay I'll do it. I'll go Above with you."

She jumped into the air, gripping his upper arm. Remembering Wren's distress, Lynx shook Tesla off, turning to point a finger in her face. "But get this straight, I am doing this for Phlox, not for you. You and I would never work out, ever, not in any world. I shouldn't even know you exist." With that he turned and walked down the alley, pretending not to care if she followed him or not.

# CHAPTER TWELVE

Tesla's mind teemed with ideas on how to accomplish her plan. She chattered along, glancing at her stone-faced companion every few moments, but Lynx remained silent as they made their way to the garden.

"This time you'll need the makeup," Tesla said, pacing in front of him. "We have to get into a meeting with my father and the others. If they find out you're a Botch beforehand, we'll never get in."

"A lot of makeup." Lynx admonished, lifting his left arm up. It was the first thing he'd said to her in several minutes.

She stopped pacing. "You're right. We need to disguise your arm altogether. You know, I heard Lilly talking about this new technology. Lilly is all about landboat racing, and *she* says that they've begun to use cuttlefish skin technology for camouflage. The cuttlefish's skin is made up of layers that are red and brown and yellow and black; below all of those is a reflective layer. The fish contracts the sacs of pigment and the effects are magnified by the reflective layer. Basically, this type of skin can change into anything we want it to." Tesla took a breath, her makeup pulsing.

"They need it for racing?"

"Lilly says that in these obstacle races, skippers need to outwit one another, not just have a fast ship. Maybe if we can get hold of a cuttlefish camo suit, we can disguise your arm."

Lynx stood up. "Where do we find it?"

Tesla looked Above at the very top windows glowing blue. "Looks like we're going to swing by the domicile and see what my sister's up to. She owes me a favor." Tesla pulled up her sleeve and typed numbers into the clear communicator on her wrist. Walking between the columns and mumbling to herself about weight capacities, she realized that Lynx wasn't beside her. He was still standing in the middle of the garden. She returned, fingertips still punching numbers, and cocked her head at him. "Something wrong?" she asked, wondering if he'd changed his mind.

"We're going to go up there, in one of those blue tube things?" he asked.

Tesla let out a chuckle which died dryly in the back of her throat. "I do believe you're scared."

"I'm not scared, I'm just trepidatious," he countered.

"Using large words won't make the fear go away," she smiled. "Tell me about it, that first trip in the Dimetrodon or whatever? Terrifying. Also, you didn't tell me the boat was going to tip over like that."

"It's called heeling and it means you're doing it right." Lynx grimaced as he looked up at the faraway windows. "And sailing a landboat is nothing like shooting through the air unprotected. Are you sure that your tiny bracelet can handle the two of us?"

"Of course I'm sure." Tesla stepped up to him and put a hand on his arm. Lynx stepped back and her hand fell from him like a cut flower. *Is it me or the transporting?* she wondered. "It's going to be just fine. There's a force field surrounding us at all times. This is cutting-edge technology, the very best." She tugged on his sleeve, finally getting him to move toward the alley again. "And really, it shouldn't be the ride up there that scares you. It should be breaking into my house."

"Thanks, Tesla, big relief there. You know, you're so good at the reassurance thing, maybe you should think about making it a career."

*A joke!* Tesla thought.

Tesla pulled Lynx over to an open area. His face was still expressionless.

"We'll have to get a little close." She felt pensive. Lynx wouldn't meet her gaze. "I'm sorry about that. About everything, really."

Lynx finally looked at her and relief surged through her as a smile, small, but a smile nonetheless crossed his face. "I know, Tesla."

"The least that I can do is try and set things right, maybe rock the boat a little bit." She jabbed him in the ribs. "Get it? Rock the boat? See what I did there?"

"Good one," Lynx said, rolling his eyes at her. "On second thought, maybe you should be in the joke business."

She threaded her arms around his waist. "Okay, Lynx, off we go."

At first, there were blue particles sparkling in the weird half-light and tugging at her clothes. A whirring, more of a vibration than a sound, started up all around them, making Tesla's lips tremble. Her braids floated around her shoulders and the hood of Lynx's sweat shirt lifted off his. Her feet lifted off the ground as the tugging sensation and whirring grew. They began to rotate as they ascended, the garden receding below them. Looking out across the jutting shapes of Middlespace, Tesla saw Lynx look down once and quickly snap his gaze back up to where they were headed. The blue beam stretched behind them like the wake of a boat. The garden fifty feet below appeared to be a small playing card, green and white with the black stone of the fountain at its center. They forged upwards toward the smooth ivory domiciles of the A-Ones.

Arriving at Tesla's home was nerve-wracking for her; knowing what her producers might do if they found Lynx made her jumpy as a cricket. But Lynx was so awed by the view he didn't look nervous at all. She yanked on his right arm so much she thought she might pull it off.

"C'mon, c'mon," she hissed, bending down in a crouch and scuttling toward the front door.

"Tes, that's not going to help you. They can still see you even if you're bent over like that. Mainly they can see how silly you look."

Tesla straightened up and stamped her foot in irritation. "We've got to get inside before they see you. Cover up your arm for Dome's sake."

"Swearing too," Lynx remarked, pivoting on the landing platform and taking in the stretch of space and sky and faraway mountains before him. "You must be really nervous. Man, this place is superb. Look at that view."

"Are you serious? Why aren't you nervous?" she asked.

He fixed her with a burning gaze. "Although I don't relish the idea of bumping into Skinner, in the end, it's your neck."

"You wouldn't say that if you knew my primary producer," Tesla warned.

Tesla was finally able to get Lynx through the giant double doors. As soon as they'd shut them, a muted beeping came from the living room.

"Tesla? Is that you?"

"Dome it all!" Tesla's eyes went wide. "The mech maid. Here! Go in here!" She grabbed the hook on the side of the wall, bearing all her weight on it. It automatically moved down the length of the hall until a doorway popped open.

"What? Where?" was all Lynx could get out before Tesla pushed him into the dark space and slammed the door shut. She spun around. The beeping sped up as the mech rolled swiftly across the foyer to her.

"X3721. Where have you been?"

Although the mech spoke in a monotone, Tesla could sense that it was suspicious.

"Avicenna's, P7764. Astronomy homework," Tesla lied. Beams of light burst from the mech maid's eyes and strafed Tesla from her face down to her waist and back up, no doubt using the built-in lie detector Skinner had installed. The mech could detect the slightest changes in breathing, heart rate, and blood pressure, all factors that fluctuated when a human lied.

*But it's a lie I told Kinsey yesterday, so maybe, just maybe ...* Tesla stood for many breathless moments as the mech evaluated her response.

The beams snapped back into the mech maid's eyes. "Adequate, X3721. Problematic but adequate. I will take it up with Producers 1 and 2 when they return within the hour. Stay in the domicile until I have done so, X3721. You will need to respond to them." With that, the mech maid pivoted and left. Tesla could hear its beeping down the hall until all was silent again.

She sagged against the wall, grabbing the hook and pulling. Lynx emerged blinking from the cramped closet, a pashmina wrapped around his head. Tesla yanked at his arm as he stumbled into the foyer.

"Hey, ouch, y'know you can be very pushy when you want to be," he said as she wrangled him across the marble-floored expanse of the foyer.

"We have to get a move on," hissed Tesla. "The mech maid bought my excuse, but who knows for how long? There is an issue of time." She hurried him down the stairs and into the living room. He slowed next to the piano, reaching out his hand as it sensed his presence and lit up.

"No!" Tesla growled, grabbing his fingers and tugging.

"Okay, okay. You know, you're the one who invited me up here. You could be a little more gracious to your date."

"Lynx!" Tesla whined as she pushed him down the hallway, the lights illuminating their path as they went. Finally they came to Tesla's doorway, where she once again shoved him out of the way as the sensor scanned her body. As soon as they were in her room, Tesla flung open the cover to a box to the right of her door, disconnecting wires haphazardly and jabbing at her communicator.

"Slow down there, you're going to strain something." Lynx sprawled on the green chaise lounge, looking as if he was utterly enjoying this.

"You wouldn't say that," Tesla said as she tugged on a stubborn wire, "if you knew my room is rigged to let Skinner know immediately if there are foreign *bodies* in here with me. He says it's to dissuade burglars but ..."

"Why didn't you say so?" He straightened up. "Get that sensor under control, missy!" Yapping erupted from underneath Tesla's bed. "What in Dome is that?"

Pav emerged, fur covered with dust bunnies. He ran up to the chaise lounge and yapped louder.

"Tesla, what *is* that thing?"

Tesla looked over from her manipulations of the sensor pad. "That's my robodog, Pav. You've never seen one? Pav, down!"

Pav ceased his shrill barking and trotted over to sit with supreme dignity at his mistress's feet. "Cute, isn't he? I guess the mech maid got him fixed, he seems better—" a bell sounded in the depths of the control panel and Pav glitched.

"Adorable," Lynx said sarcastically.

"Aha!" Tesla said, shutting the door to the sensory pad. "That should do it. I think we're safe. At least until Skinner comes home and reprograms the dang thing."

Lynx squatted down in front of Pav, stretching out his human hand for the robodog to smell. Pav turned his nose up, refusing to sniff, and turned his back to Lynx. "Like I said, adorable," Lynx quipped.

Tesla stood in front of a wall and said, "Reflection." The wall shimmered and turned reflective. "This might give us an idea of how that camo-suit will look before we go to the trouble of procuring one." She led Lynx in front of the wall and stood beside him. "Cuttle camo," she said to the wall. The wall flickered and their two reflections disappeared. "Huh, that doesn't work."

She stepped aside and said, "Cuttle camo programmed as an A-One." Lynx's reflection reappeared and now he stood in the basic uniform of an A-One: muted colors, tailored cut, no patterns, and, most importantly, his left arm appeared normal. Awed, Lynx raised it, glancing at the real metal one hanging in the air before him, and then back at his image in the mirror.

"That'll do," Tesla said. "Now to chime Lilly." She began typing once again on her communicator. "I'll tell her to come to my room. We don't want to reprogram her sensor pad too."

"This is so cool," Lynx was moving his metal arm back and forth in front of the mirror. "Can I tell it anything?"

"Lynx, this isn't a game."

"Please, Tes?"

"All right, but let's make it quick. What do you want to look like?"

"Full botch, all modifications."

"Well then," Tesla said, and to the wall, "All parts metallic."

Lynx's image shimmered again and this time he reappeared completely made of metal. Even his head and face were different parts of metal. He opened his mouth and stuck out his tongue. In the mirror a scaly silvery tongue poked out between thin twisted wire lips.

"So that's what it will be like," he said.

"What what'll be like?"

"Phlox, when everything's metal, when the plague finally takes all her parts."

Tesla paused in her typing and met his eyes in the mirror; even in his metallic reflection, Tesla could still see the confusion and dismay in his gaze. She waved a hand in front of the mirror, turning it into a non-reflective wall once again, and faced Lynx. "That's not going to happen to Phlox."

"Says you."

"We can do it, Lynx." She caught his metal hand in both of hers. He looked at her for a long moment and then nodded. A chime sounded above the doorway and a silhouette appeared behind the smoky plastic door. "Time to cash in a favor."

A few moments later Tesla stood in between Lynx and Lilly.

"Lynx, Lilly; Lilly, Lynx," Tesla was saying with exasperation.

"Omidomeomidomeomidome." Lilly's normally large eyes were even larger. "Really Tesla? This is your big secret? I knew you were hiding something but I thought it was like you got a less than perfect on a test or didn't win the regional in your aikido tournament, not that your new boyfriend is an Underdweller!"

"Botch," Lynx stated. He had a funny look on his face, as if he were trying to remember something.

"Wow, of course, Botch." Lilly sat on the bed, mouth agape, black lace skirt ballooning around her knees. "This is so cool. Seriously, I've never been more proud to be your sister. Look at his arm! That is so chive."

"Lilly, cool it." Tesla looked at Lynx. "I'm sorry."

He nodded and grimaced, shifting from one foot to the other under Lilly's scrutiny, still wearing his befuddled expression. "Tes, you mentioned that she looked like Phlox. Man, does she. Except for her coloring. But her features ..." He trailed off, his expression confused.

"Lilly, Lilly, LILLY!" Tesla shouted in her sister's face.

Lilly finally focused on Tesla's face and closed her mouth. "What?"

"We need your help," Tesla enunciated each word.

"My help?"

"Yes, Lilly. I'm asking you for that favor."

"Okay," Lilly said slowly.

"We need a camo-suit, you know, like one of those new ones. A camo cuttle suit."

This got Lilly's attention. "You need a what now? What for?"

"Can't tell you that, Sis. Listen, are you going to help us or what?"

Lilly thought for a moment, one bright pink stiletto tapping on Tesla's pearl gray carpeting. "We'll have to go to the Bottom."

"You know about the Bottom?" Lynx sounded surprised.

"Of course I know about the Bottom, I'm not a total digger, like my sister here." Lilly jerked her head in Tesla's direction and winked at Lynx.

"This was a total waste of time," Tesla said, moving toward her door.

"Wait, no!" Lilly held her hands up. "I know a guy who'll get you one of those things. I'll have to go with you because I'm the one he knows. He's a bit of a tweaker that one. I mean you could try and go yourself," Lilly said, playing with the ribbons that wound through her elbow-length black gloves. "There's no telling if he'll let you in. He may even vaporize you for your trouble. Me on the other hand, he and I go way back. He'll totally listen to me."

Tesla sighed, "I don't think we have a choice. Okay, Lilly, you can come with us."

"Awesome!" She jumped up and did a little jig in the middle of the room, making Pav glitch out, only to reappear with his tongue lolling.

"Quit it, you're upsetting the dog."

"Right, sorry, when do we leave?"

"Immediately."

"We're not all going in one of those beam thingies," Lynx began. "Not all of us together." He made a squishing motion with his hands.

"No, that won't do," Tesla said, putting her finger to her mouth. "We're too heavy."

Suddenly Lilly snapped her fingers, "I know, let's go in my boat, the Parvicursor. Par One for short. Tes, I'll finally get you on the Par One. You're going to love it!"

Tesla groaned.

"Wait, how do we get to the ground, you know, to sail the boat?" Lynx asked.

Lilly's grin widened. "Why we fly, of course. We fly. Now, if I can just make sure we won't crash from the excess weight."

Tesla groaned again as Lilly went to retrieve her boat.

# CHAPTER THIRTEEN

hen Lilly returned, it became clear that she stored the Par
One in a bottle.

"It's in that?" Lynx asked. Mounted inside was a tiny boat, one that looked a lot like the landboats Lynx was used to sailing, but much cooler. It was translucent with magenta racing stripes down the side. It had an oblong shape with sharp wings jutting from each side and one protruding from the roof, making the whole contraption look like a snub-nosed shark.

Lilly handed it over to Lynx, who promptly shook it, causing Lilly to screech and snatch it back. "Careful!" Lilly hugged the bottle to her chest.

Tesla returned from the bathroom. She had changed into black jeans and a black T-shirt, with a bright red, long-sleeved shirt underneath. Her face was free of the glowing makeup. "I can see now why you were so concerned about fitting us all in there." She'd released her hair from the braids, and it tumbled down her back in loose waves. She was brushing through it with her fingertips when she caught Lynx staring. "What?"

He inclined his head toward her body.

"I changed. So what? I wanted to look the part. You know, tough."

"I hate to fill you in, Sis, but wearing black is not going to make

Gunther think that you know what you're doing. That's where I come in. And don't worry about the Par One, she's quite roomy once you get inside. Hey, what's with your door?" Lilly was at the door, waving a hand in front of the sensor.

"Oh that," Tesla said. "It's nothing, just a glitch." She strode over to the panel, hip-checking it, and the door slid open. "Pav, stay. Deactivate."

Pav crumpled to the floor with a whine, eyes darkening.

"Let's go," Tesla said, typing into her communicator. "I'll program both our rooms to be on sleep mode. That way, when our producers or the mech maid come by, they'll think we're simply asleep."

"Not bad, little sister. No wonder you're the one they have all their hopes and dreams pinned on. Not that it bothers me," Lilly said over her shoulder to Lynx. "I enjoy living up to other people's low expectations. Sometimes I even exceed them, just for kicks. But not too often."

Lynx and Lilly followed Tesla across the darkened living room, the sweep of starlit mountains stretching out beyond the windows. A tornado was whipping in from the west. At the moment it was just a distant cone racing across the desert floor, but within an hour it would stretch to twice the height of the Dome.

A beeping noise floated down the hallway.

"The mech maid!" Tesla hissed from the foyer. "Come on, Lynx!"

Lynx bounded the three stairs up from the living room as Tesla threw the front door open. He tripped on the final step, causing both girls to gasp. The living room glowed from the mech maid's approaching bio-electric lights as Lynx picked himself up and hurtled over the last step. The beeping grew louder as the three hurried out into the evening air. When the doors closed behind them, the two sisters sagged with relief.

"Who is the mech maid anyways?" Lynx asked.

"It's a mechanical maid, our domestic," Tesla answered.

"A domestic mech, huh?"

"Something like that," Lilly agreed as she placed the small boat next to her pink-toed foot. "Except Daddy Dearest programmed it to be his watchdog."

Lilly pulled a vial on a chain out of her shirt. She extracted a dropper from it and held it over the tiny boat. "Back up y'all, you don't want to get in the way of this." She squeezed the dropper. A crackling noise filled the air, along with the scent of creosote, and then, with a twang as if many guitar strings were snapping at once, the boat sprang to full size, towering over them.

"Epic," Lynx said in awe.

Lilly squealed in delight and trotted over to her boat, standing on tiptoe and hugging it. She looked back to see both Lynx and Tesla staring at her. "What? I missed her."

Lilly punched buttons on her communicator and the top hatch sprung open as the rungs of a ladder appeared on the hull of the boat. She leapt onto the lowest rung, ascending the ladder in her high heels with surprising speed. She disappeared into the cockpit, and in a moment pink and yellow running lights came on along the ship's wings. A hum started up in the hatch as Lilly's head popped up over the side. "Well, come on, you slowpokes! Primary producers one and two may be home any minute."

Tesla and Lynx climbed up the side of the ship. The cockpit had two seats up front and a storage area behind. The controls spread out in front of Lilly, who was buckling herself into a day-glo yellow harness.

"Safety first, but fashion a close second. Lynx, you're up front with me. Tesla, you're in back. There's an extra harness behind that handbag."

Tesla sighed and stretched her legs up and over, settling

in behind the driver's side and moving a turquoise handbag to uncover a purple harness. Lynx seated himself next to Lilly who was flicking switches and twisting dials; at one point she pressed her palm against a touchscreen. The ship shuddered and lifted a few feet into the air. A final twist of a dial drew the clear roof up and over their heads with a shush and a click. "Locked and loaded. Let's go downtown, way way way downtown," Lilly said.

Fitting her hands into two raised circular ports, Lilly maneuvered the ship up and off the oval of their domicile's landing pad. They hovered for a few moments. Lilly looked over at Lynx and threw him a wink as she urged the ship into a controlled drop toward the lower levels of the Dome. They avoided transporter beams and dodged around the towers and building extensions of Middlespace. They were nearing the ground when Lilly pulled the Par One up and flew it parallel, zigging and zagging around crowds and hovercarts. Tesla shrieked from the back and kept up a steady stream of admonishments, pointing out to Lilly every possible collision.

"Tesla, I mean this in the nicest way possible, but could you please shut it? I've done this, like, a million times before," Lilly said while going up and over the gates of a carnival. She dodged around a holographic carousel and headed straight for a cart selling deep-fried grubs. Tesla went silent in the back, although as they just missed the grub cart, she let out a little whimper.

Up ahead yawned a large opening with the words "Tunnel of Love" blinking in fluorescent tubing. Lilly slowed her speed by a fraction as they disappeared inside.

"Just the place for you lovebirds," she remarked, leaning forward in concentration. She flew at a height of about fifteen feet, just high enough to clear the automatic boats peopled by astonished riders, who looked up as the Par One's pink and yellow lights swooshed overhead. The ship zigged and zagged around corners at nausea-inducing velocity; with the ship's speed the grinning cupids that lined the dark tunnel morphed into sneering satyrs.

"Lilly? Lilly?" Lynx gripped his armrests, watching as a fork in the tunnel approached at a furious velocity. "LILLY?!"

"You too?" Lilly smirked. "Oh ye of little faith." She jerked the console to the right, pulling them away from the glowing hearts of the Tunnel of Love. When the headlights snapped on, it became apparent that they were in a maintenance tunnel of some sort. Rusted pipes ran overhead and the windshield was splattered with whatever viscous material the pipes carried. The Par One angled downward until a smallish oval of light appeared up ahead. They soon flew into a cavernous room with an orange octagon painted on the floor, orange lines radiating in all directions and with an indelicate thump, the Par One landed on the Bottom.

Lilly turned around in her seat. "Ladies, gentlemen, and mechs, we have arrived at our final destination," she intoned in a high-pitched voice as she pressed buttons and the roof retracted. "Please make sure to kiss your captain on the way out."

Tesla made an exasperated noise from the back. "All these years you've been trying to get me into this bucket of bolts, and you know what?" She swung her leg over the seat and pulled herself out of the Par One. Her pale face popped back over the edge of the cockpit. "Never again!" Then she dropped out of sight.

"Well, that's just ridiculous," Lilly said as she unbuckled her harness. "I mean, how does she expect to get back up there, walk?"

Lynx freed himself from his constricting harness. "Thanks for the ride, Lilly. I enjoyed it. Mostly." He pulled himself up and over the lip of the cockpit. Tesla was on the ground next to the Par One, looking around in wonder. The Bottom was the guts of the Dome and looked like a robotic catacomb. All of the infrastructure was based here. Gigantic pipes pulled fresh water from the outer Rim. The wiring and other essentials that kept the A-Ones comfortable at the top of their personal palaces all started down here. Alleys branched out like spokes on a wheel from the orange octagon. Each one was lined with storefronts; the makeshift windows were curtained and shuttered, with a sign and a different color lightbulb hanging outside.

"This is the one." Lilly started down one of the alleyways. "Once I introduce you to Gunther, I'm going to do some shopping." They made their way down the dank lane. If Lynx had wanted to, he could have reached up and touched the gritty ceiling.

On their way, they passed a few pedestrians unlike anyone Lynx had ever seen before. One woman exiting a shop had spikes embedded in her face and two horns pushing through her forehead. Lynx couldn't help but stare after her, noticing a tail protruding from the bottom of her mini skirt.

Lilly, striding ahead, pointed out what each doorway had to offer.

"Opium den, satanists, virtual realities, computer viruses sold in bulk. Yep, they have it all down here. What did you all bring for trade?"

"Two currbytes," supplied Tesla.

Lilly let out a low whistle, glancing at her sister with a new respect. "And how, may I ask, did you come by those?"

"Some secrets I keep to myself, Lill," Tesla said with a small smile.

"Obviously," Lilly agreed, gesturing at Lynx's tall form striding beside her. "Here we are."

Lilly stepped up to a black door where a sign inscribed with a "$\mathcal{G}$" swung askew off one of its hinges. The red lightbulb above their heads blinked on and off. Lilly paused in front of the door, biting her bottom lip. She raised one gloved hand and knocked a complicated tattoo on the door in front of her. After a few moments, it creaked open and an eye appeared in the crack. Lilly whispered something through the door. It shut in her face, she stepped back in surprise, and then it swung open wide. Lilly walked in and Tesla and Lynx followed.

Holding the door open was a woman unimaginably tall and thin. She swayed back and forth as her long fingers beckoned to them. Her skin was a light violet and her eyes slanted up toward her temples, so far that they seemed to disappear into the orange hair that hung down to her waist. She wore a gossamer dress belted with a chain that flowed to her ankles. The fabric was printed with a moving swirling pattern; Lynx couldn't look at it for long without feeling as if he was falling into a trance.

She led them into a hallway papered in flocked red velvet and hung with portraits of strange-looking people: some as thin and elongated as their guide, others hugely fat with double eyes and multiple chins, and a few looking as if they were half human and half animal. All the eyes in the portraits followed them as they walked to the doorway covered with the same velvet.

"What is she?" Lynx whispered to Lilly.

"Sylph," she threw back over her shoulder, never taking her eyes off the form ahead of her. "Has a bad habit of disappearing so keep her in view. It's extreme body modification to make her look like an elemental. She's as human as you or me."

The sylph reached the curtain and pulled it open with a violet finger, gesturing toward the room beyond with her other hand. When Lynx passed her, he could see that her eyes were as orange as her hair, and that they each had not one, but two pupils. "Thanks," Lynx said. The sylph didn't respond.

The large circular room was stuffed with books, filling bookcases on nearly every wall, piled in towers that almost reached the twenty-foot ceiling, covering every conceivable surface except for the large four-poster bed in the center of the room. This was occupied by an enormous man, or what Lynx thought was a man.

His jet black skin glowed as though it had been oiled. His blonde hair was combed back from his dark forehead and his eyes were of the lightest blue. "Welcome," he boomed as the trio walked over to his bedside. "Please excuse me if I don't get up. It's more trouble than it's worth."

"Gunther." Lilly leaned down and air-kissed to the right and left of the man's face. "This is my sister, Tesla."

Lilly grabbed Tesla's forearm and yanked her close to the bed. "Charmed," Tesla said.

"And her buddy, Lynx. He's an Underdweller," she said to Gunther in a mock whisper. Lynx rolled his eyes and stepped forward. He looked at the giant propped against a mound of silk pillows. "Nice to meet you."

"It's always nice to meet family and friends of my number one customer." Gunther grinned at Lilly, his white teeth a sharp contrast against his coal black skin.

"Are these real books?" Lynx inquired, looking in wonder at the stacks.

"Yes. I prefer the real to the electronic version."

"Right, well, I want to go scour the Bottom for some things I need." Lilly headed for the hallway. "See you guys in, say, thirty minutes by the Par One, okay?"

"Sure," Tesla agreed, glancing at her communicator. "Thirty minutes."

"Give them a good deal, Gunther. They're family," Lilly said as she walked toward the doorway.

When the curtain swished behind Lilly, Gunther boomed, "What can I do for the two of you?"

"We need a cuttle camo suit," Lynx said.

At that Gunther's eyebrows went up. "Really? Lilly usually wants frivolities to purchase. What would you want something like that for?"

This time Tesla spoke up. "We need to disguise Lynx here as an A-One."

Gunther didn't move. He didn't even blink. Suddenly, the only book-free wall slid upward into the ceiling, revealing another room humming with electricity and bright with artificial light. Another man stepped out of the room. He was short and bald, with tattoos running across his skull and over his eyes.

"Thank you, Igor. That will be all," he said to the man on the bed. He turned to Tesla and Lynx. "Good evening. I am Gunther."

# CHAPTER FOURTEEN

ynx and Tesla looked back and forth between the two figures. "I let Igor here conduct most of my business," the bald man said. "The majority of my customers are much like your sister: easily satisfied. Will you please come into my office?"

The real Gunther spun on his heel; Lynx and Tesla followed him into the room. Lynx looked over his shoulder before the wall came back down and gave Igor a wave as the man picked up a book again.

Gunther's real office was floor-to-ceiling panels, some superimposed over others. He seated himself at a lucite desk that had touchscreens and keyboards mounted at different heights all across it.

"Sit," he said, motioning toward the space in front of the desk. Two round chairs instantly emerged out of the floor. "You're looking for a cuttle camo suit. What necessitates this young man disguising himself as an A-One?" Gunther steepled his fingers as his tattoos gyrated across his forehead in the same manner as the sylph's dress.

Tesla leaned forward in her seat. "Lynx and I are going to try and meet with the top programmers. I want him as proof to show them that Botches are human."

Gunther's eyebrows raised. "Interesting. It is my understanding that A-Ones keep their products separate from everyone else in the Dome so that they won't discover the social discrepancies. Normally the only contact between Underdwellers, Middlespacers, and A-Ones is at the races. Or down here." He grinned, revealing pointed teeth.

Tesla continued, glancing at Lynx warily. "We met in Middlespace."

Lynx took up the thread. "She saved me from getting vaporized. Then she made me promise to take her Below."

Gunther leaned back in his chair. "And the cuttle camo suit?"

"He can't go Above as an Underdweller. If I can get him into a meeting with Skinner and the other programmers, maybe we can make them change their thinking and then they'll find a way to stop the plague," Tesla said. "I have to do something. I am X3721 after all. I may be young but I have that."

Gunther sighed. "There's nothing like the idealism of youth. Your dedication to a group whose very existence you are not supposed to know about is impressive. I doubt you will succeed but betting on the winning team is not why I'm in this business." He stared at Tesla. "What do you have to trade?"

Tesla tapped some numbers into her communicator, showing them to Gunther when she'd finished. He leaned back, disappointment evident in his face. "I am sorry, but that is not sufficient. No currency would be." He stood, walking toward the doorway with his hand outspread. "We've reached an impasse. I will show you out."

"Wait!" Tesla threw Lynx a desperate glance. "What about a currbyte?"

Gunther stopped walking but didn't turn around. The tattoos' swirling sped up, pulsing up and over the glistening skin of his skull. *I wonder if his tattoos work like Tesla's makeup, speeding up when he gets agitated,* Lynx thought.

After a silence of a minute or more, Tesla conceded. "Two

currbytes." A pause stretched between the three people; it was so complete that Lynx could hear Gunther's computers humming.

Finally, Gunther spun and walked back to his desk. "That's more like it. Here's what I'll do: two suits for that price, the last one, not the first. It's for the same reason that I let you into my office."

Tesla's mouth dropped open. "Two suits, why that's, that's fantastic. Thank you."

"It was I who created the technology, so let's say this joint venture will benefit all of us. I think we will be hearing about your attempt at equalizing the social scale quite soon, X3721, successful or not. And I plan on having everyone know that it was my cuttle camo suit that allowed it to happen." Gunther walked over to a wall, punching numbers on his own black communicator. A door slid upwards to reveal a storage room lined with boxes and lumpy packages. He stepped into the room, returning in a minute with two garment bags, which he laid out on the desk. He unzipped one and pulled out a shimmering bodysuit.

"It will sync to your unique voice register. All you have to do is depress this button." He turned over the cuff of the glittery suit where a small portion rose a millimeter, individuating an oval from the rest of the fabric. "Then speak clearly and the suit will respond, changing to look like anything you like. There is also a hood, which can be deployed by pulling this string." Gunther drew their attention to a silver thread that hung off the collar. "That way you can be in full camo. Let's see you try one on."

He threw a suit at Lynx, who caught it, sliding the slippery fabric between his fingertips. Gunther handed Tesla the other. "Why don't you change in the storeroom?" She walked into the storage area and Gunther retracted the door.

Lynx sloughed off his clothes and pulled the material, which felt like oiled snakeskin, over his body while Gunther continued to tell him about the suit's properties.

"It's breathable, always a good option, and although it fits like a glove, it will appear as if it has the dimensions of normal clothing. Part of the technology I created."

Lynx pulled up the zipper on the side of his suit.

"Try it," Gunther prodded.

Lynx pushed the oval in the inside of the cuff and said, "Light blue shirt, dark brown pants." When he looked down at himself, he was dressed in the clothes he had specified, simple and with no embellishment. "Bullseye on the front of the shirt," he added, remembering to hit the button. A bullseye shimmered into being on the front of his shirt, which billowed and hung exactly how a real shirt would.

"Now the most important part. Try the arm," Gunther urged.

Lynx nodded, pushing the small button once again. "Left arm, full flesh." The metal that stretched the light blue material of his shirt shimmered again and a perfectly human arm appeared.

"You'll still be able to utilize the modifications in your arm," Gunther said. Lynx detached the fingertip of his pointer finger and fired up the laser. It looked strange, a human finger emitting a blue flame, but there it was.

The storage room door opened up and Tesla strode out dressed in black as she'd been before. "I thought you were going to try it on?" Lynx asked her, as she pulled at the neck of her t-shirt. Tesla smiled, pressing the button on her wrist. "Full ballgown," she said. "Sea green." The black outfit shimmered and suddenly Tesla was standing before them in a teal evening dress.

"Very clever," Gunther said, smiling. Tesla swept a curtsey to them both. "And now for the most important part of the transaction: payment."

"Right," Tesla said, and punched numbers into her communicator. "What's your transfer code?" she asked Gunther, inputting the information as he gave it to her. "There, it's done."

"Splendid," Gunther said, rubbing his hands together. "I wish you success in your attempt to bring balance to the Dome. But even if you fail, remember to tell them where you got your suits."

When Lynx and Tesla reached the Par One, it was locked and Lilly nowhere to be found, but they didn't mind, so enthralled were they by the properties of their new suits. When they asked the suits to match their backgrounds and they were hooded, Tesla and Lynx were invisible except for a slight bulging of the outlines of whatever was behind them.

They could hear Lilly long before they saw her, high heels clip-clopping down an alley to their left. Lynx winked at Tesla, pressing the button and whispering "match background" to his suit as he pulled the hood up. Tesla smiled and did the same. Lilly came around the back of the Par One, laden with some impressive-looking packages and sporting a pair of sunglasses whose lenses looked as if they had spider webs attached to the front of them. She was five feet from them when she stopped.

"Nice try, guys," she called out as she typed into her communicator, popping the hatch to the Par One. "Why do you think I picked up a pair of body heat shades?"

Tesla sighed and said "default outfit" to the cuff while Lynx pulled back his hood, looking like a disembodied floating head.

Lilly grinned at them both and then scaled the side of the ship, packages balanced awkwardly on her shoulder. Once they were all settled in their seats, the Par One humming and hovering off the ground, Lilly looked at them and asked, "Obviously Gunther's was a success. Anything to say to me?"

"Yeah," said Tesla from the back. "Try not to kill us on the way back up."

Lilly hit the throttle.

They dropped Lynx off at the bank of elevators, with directives to meet up the next afternoon in the garden. It was late, very late indeed, but Tesla would try and schedule a meeting with the top programmers before reconvening with him the next day. Whizzing back toward home on the top of the elevator, Lynx was surprised to find that he missed her. They had been together for almost ten consecutive hours, but here he was, tired and footsore, and he missed her. As uncomfortable as he was with the situation, life would be very dull indeed if an A-One named Tesla hadn't stuck her neck out for him in what felt like aeons ago.

# CHAPTER FIFTEEN

Lynx made sure that his tasks the next morning took him away from the pod and, specifically, away from Wren's pointed questions. He assumed that she would not approve of their plan to disrupt the Dome's social order, as much as she disagreed with the system that was currently in place. For most of the morning and the beginning of the afternoon, he was checking the electrical shortcuts on the grid.

One quick glance outside confirmed that the fair weather that he and Tesla had frolicked in was a precursor to a set of superstorms. Last night's tornado had been the smallest to come through, and all this morning Lynx had been working next to a view of mustard-colored mist, at times billowing into a darker orange, spitting sand against the glass.

One o'clock found him racing through the Waterworks toward the center of the Dome. He'd had to change into the body-hugging camo suit in the antechamber of the wastewaters. He arrived at the garden at a little past two, panting and hoping he wasn't too sweaty. Tesla was already there, dressed in billowing gray pants and a white shirt. She was perched on the side of the pool, circling one fingertip in the water and watching the excited reaction of the fish. When she looked up and fixed him with her gray-green gaze, everything else around him fell away.

"Hi," he said tensely.

"Hi," Tesla said with a nervous grin.

They were a little wary of each other. It was a contradictory sensation. While Lynx wanted to be around her (the torture of the last hours without her company was testament to that) he also felt jumpy and ungainly, tripping over the raised cobblestones as they walked between the columns. His heart tripled its beats as she slid her arms around him and craned her neck to see behind him as she tapped into her communicator. The air began to sparkle and pulse blue around them, and Tesla's hair, loose today, lifted into a glittering sheet. The vibration started up and Lynx felt weightlessness take over.

"Listen," Tesla had to shout to be heard over the hum that enveloped them. "I've set it all up. It'll be Skinner, that's my primary producer, and possibly one other programmer. I've told them that your name is Locke and that you're a classmate of mine and we're doing a project on programming and need to interview them. Sounds tight, wouldn't you say?"

"Sounds solid." The vibration tickled his vocal cords. "Tes, you really think this will work? I mean, the chances that they're all of sudden going to change their minds about us is kind of slim, y'know?" Doubt and worry began to creep into Lynx's mind.

Tesla looked into his eyes, pulling him closer as she did. "We have to try, Lynx. We can't let it go on like this. And maybe, just maybe, it will help find a cure for the plague."

They were transporting to a new part of the A-Ones' quarters at the top of the Dome. Instead of going to one of the branches, they were headed for the thick trunk of the core. Hundreds and hundreds of bubbled windows stippled the white exterior, opening into the air with a balcony and sometimes a landing pad. As they got closer, Lynx could see the white and gray coats of the programmers, their blinking and glowing screens highlighting their features.

"Almost there. It's a good thing we got here before Rain-time," Tesla remarked.

They had crested the whole of the superstructure. The view that stretched out before Lynx was unlike any he'd ever had the pleasure of seeing before, and this time, he did not fear the height. He looked down between the branches of the A-Ones' living spaces, through to the mismatched dwellings of the Middlespacers and patches of ground. The bustle of tiny people looked like a moving, living carpet or an underwater seabed of scintillating seaweed.

His view was eclipsed as they moved up and over the lip of a landing pad. The transporter lowered them to the surface and, as their feet touched down, the beam dissolved in a shower of sparks. They were at the very top of the supercity, across from a white building shaped like half a pentagon. One tinted rectangular window sat in the middle, and smaller triangular ones framed it, tapering down to nothing.

Lynx and Tesla looked at each other and she held out her hand to him. He squeezed it once and then let go. As they approached the building, a rectangular doorway slid upwards, revealing an oval room with nothing but a podium in the middle staffed by a mech with blue skin using a touchscreen computer. It looked the pair over without expression as they approached.

"Yes," it said with no inflection at all.

Tesla stepped up. "I am X3721, and I have an appointment to interview KG727."

The mech turned its yellow gaze down to the handheld tablet and placed one finger on it. The mech's eyes, half-lidded and unseeing, widened, turning translucent as a line of 0's and 1's unfurled across each iris's surface.

"You may proceed." It inclined its head backwards. Two doors opened into another oval room with an identical set of windows. As they walked around the mech's podium, Lynx glanced back to see that it had no lower body; wires connected it to the podium itself.

"Basically, it's like a computer with a face," Tesla said. "Skinner probably could've simply installed a touchscreen, but he likes to show off a bit."

This next room had a horseshoe-shaped table stretching for twenty feet in front of the bank of tinted windows, which darkened and intensified the sun's purply rays. Large screens bracketed the table and two figures were seated behind it. It took a moment for Lynx's eyes to adjust to the gloomy atmosphere, but when he did, he was surprised to recognize one of the people there. He stopped short next to Tesla, whose arm, next to his, was tense.

"Mendel," he whispered.

Tesla pulled her shoulders back and strode to the center of the room, unfazed by this turn of events. She seated herself on one of the two chairs that had been pulled, like taffy, from the dark blue carpeting.

"Good afternoon," Tesla said, all business. "I appreciate your coming together like this, and on such short notice. I am X3721, better known to my familiars as Tesla, and this is P6392, known to his friends as Locke." Tesla glanced at Lynx, and he saw the fear in her eyes. She jerked her gaze sideways, glancing at Mendel before turning back to the table in front of them.

"Locke, I am Skinner, top programmer here in the Dome and also, by happenstance, Tesla's primary producer. The man next to me is Mendel, one of the most brilliant programmers of all time. Without him, none of this would've been possible. I thought it would be helpful to have Mendel here to describe some of the intricacies of our process."

Lynx looked expectantly toward Mendel, but their tour guide of the pollinator dome seemed to have been replaced by someone quite different. Eyes half-lidded and mustache drooping, he gave both Lynx and Tesla a curt nod before turning his attention back to Skinner.

Tesla cleared her throat. "We are here because we've been studying the infrastructure of the Dome, about how you programmers run it and condition it. We thought we'd come to the primary source for certain angles of our report. Now then, first question: how did the A-Ones come to be?"

"As you know," Skinner began, "A-Ones are genetically perfect. It took years to cultivate our own genetic strands and a lot of trial and error. Of course, even being genetically perfect, there are certain inevitabilities that we cannot escape: illness, injury, death."

"How did you propose to solve these sizable issues?" Tesla asked.

"Normally I wouldn't be so forthcoming about our system but today is special," Skinner paused, his chest puffed out and cheeks flushed with pride. "We created a race of people, well to be fair Mendel did although I also contributed indispensably to the project. These people are genetic copies of ourselves."

Lynx instantly tensed in his chair; next to him he heard Tesla suck in her breath. *A race of clones?* "Why would you need a race of clones? And where do you keep them?" he asked.

Skinner looked at him critically. "We keep them right here in the Dome. If an A-One needs a part—they chop off their finger, need an organ replacement, develop an unsightly rash—then the pairing gene, once activated, will alert harvesters to the presence of the correct specimen, and will render that specimen immobile and unaware during the procedure. For now we keep them close: Below."

Realization and rage washed over Lynx's mind. *He's talking about us, Botches, or better yet, Spare Parts! Phlox! Oh, Phlox.* Grief flooded his mind as he struggled to stay still.

Beside him, Tesla was leaning forward in her seat, abject horror written in her furrowed brow, clenched jaw, and balled fists. "You mean that when Lilly needed a new arm, you didn't grow it? It came from her clone? Tell me this isn't true!"

"Of course it's true," Skinner was nonchalantly cleaning his nails. "We couldn't have your sister walking around without an arm, now could we? We embed memories of a virus or illness as well as a whiff of amnesia to explain for their missing parts. It's the least we can do; we wouldn't want an uprising on our hands."

*That explains why I can't remember anything that happened before Wren took us in,* Lynx thought as he struggled to control his facial features.

"The plague. They think the plague takes their parts," whispered Tesla.

"There you have it," Skinner answered. "The system works perfectly."

"You cannot be serious! This the most horrible thing I've ever … and you say the Botches don't have feelings! This is inhumane, it's worse than that … it's, it's evil!" Tesla's face was dead white except for the two spots of color high on her cheekbones. "Everything you've ever taught me is a LIE!"

"Now, now, Tes. Don't get yourself all worked up. It's what they're made for." Skinner stared at his daughter, surprised at her outrage.

Lynx had to suppress an urge to whip out his left hand and blast the loser's face off. "And what about the clones?" Lynx asked through gritted teeth. "Is there any consideration of their feelings?"

Skinner cocked his head at Lynx and started to chuckle, which then became whooping guffaws. Mendel didn't join in, his expressionless face even more coma-like. Skinner had to wipe his eyes with a handkerchief before he could respond to Lynx's question.

"My dear boy," he said, mopping his reddened cheeks. "Haven't you been paying any attention to your lessons? Underdwellers don't have any emotions, at least not any emotions that matter. We bred it out of them. And it will matter even less in a few weeks."

Lynx couldn't trust himself to speak. He was so consumed with horror and anger, pure searing hate for all of them and the world he had been born into to serve other humans only as a way for them to maintain physical perfection. He was glad to hear Tesla's trembling voice. "What do you mean by that?"

"Well, I probably shouldn't say anything, but you will find out soon anyway. It seems as though we won't be needing the Underdwellers at all in a short while. We can use them up at any rate we want. We've been contacted, no, *I* have been contacted by a force outside the Dome." Lynx's anger was momentarily quelled by a spurt of surprise at this revelation.

"This force calls itself Axios. It's an absolute breakthrough because it proves that there is life beyond the Dome," Skinner continued. "Axios has plans for us to be part of a bigger experiment. It has requested that we make ourselves available. Think of it! Finally A-Ones will be able to collude with a force that is deserving of our genetics and intelligence. We are finally moving on to the next phase!" His enthusiasm was met with silence.

Mendel perked up, sitting up straighter and blinking a few times as if he were waking from a long sleep.

"I say, what what?"

Lynx had to suppress another urge, this time to scream "What!?!?" right back at him, not in humor but out of pure confusion at the injustice of it all. Mendel addressed Skinner. "Skinner, sir, don't you think that is a little rash? Axios needs to be corroborated before we go any further."

"I thought I'd meet with resistance. That's why I've arranged to have my own product taken as their first guest. And today, believe it or not. What an honor!" He gestured toward Tesla.

Mendel turned his gaze toward the two youths sitting before them. "Luna? But that's impossible! She's one of them, like him."

Skinner looked from Lynx and Tesla and back to Mendel.

"Yes, I know Mendel. They are both A-Ones, like us. My dear sir, I feel as if you've had your mind wiped one too many times."

"What, wait, what?" Mendel spat back. "What do you mean mind wipe? And they're both Underdwellers! She's had half her skull replaced and him, well, look at his arm!"

Skinner turned infinitely slowly to stare at Lynx's hand. Lynx stood, no longer able to contain himself. "You can't do this to us. You can't use us up, like a bucket of bolts! We're human! We have families! We love and hurt and live and die, as much as you do!" He unhinged his hand and blasted a freeze ray at the two surprised people in front of him.

"Lynx, no!" Tesla yelled, jumping up and holding out her hands to stop him. The icy ray shot out of the end of Lynx's wrist and ricocheted off a force field in front of the table, occluding the image of the two programmers rising to their feet, aghast. The ray splashed against the invisible wall in front of them and, like a flood of dry ice, curled up and over to engulf Lynx and Tesla.

It felt as if every cell of Lynx's body suddenly had a rime of ice engulfing it. He could still breathe and move his eyes around, but just barely. *Well that was stupid,* he thought. Tesla was frozen in her posture of protest, mouth open in a shout, hands outstretched, eyes pleading.

"A basic protecto-field. I thought you would've known that those are standard issue, *Locke*." Sarcasm dripped from the name. "But you wouldn't, would you, not if you aren't a real A-One. And Tesla. Tesla, Tesla, Tesla," scolded Skinner, making his way down to where his daughter stood frozen.

"My dear, so disappointing! Don't you realize what an honor it is to be chosen? How this is our personal invitation to join a force that may have *been the creator of us in the first place!*"

"Surely you can't think that," said a shocked Mendel, hand over his heart.

"Can and do," replied a bemused Skinner. "It makes logical sense. A true scientist would recognize that," he scoffed, reaching out to caress Tesla's face with his forefinger. Tesla's eyes were rapidly switching between Lynx and Skinner. "It's such an honor, my dear, and I am delighted to say that they asked for you by production code, that they wanted you *specifically*. I knew I hit the mark when I made your strand, X3721, I just didn't realize what the mark was at the time."

Out of his pocket, Skinner drew a black tool the size and shape of a pen, but with no nib. "And as for that arm of yours, boy, with its fancy weaponry? We have toys just like it." Skinner pushed the end of the small black tube and it began to throb purple until it shot out a ray which quickly engulfed Tesla in glowing netting. Skinner raised the tube, and Tesla, still frozen, rose with it. "Thank you, Locke," Skinner said over his shoulder, keeping his concentration pinned on the floating girl as he moved around the conference table. "It seems you've done the job of immobilizing her for transportation for me."

Skinner pressed his free hand against a touchpad to the left of the bank of windows and the middle window slid up to reveal another landing pad, on which sat a larger and even more tricked-out version of the Par One. Mendel threw a guilty glance at Lynx and scurried after Skinner.

"Oh and *Locke*, stick around until I return." With that Skinner broke up into gales of laughter as the window slid down again.

# CHAPTER SIXTEEN

t felt like hours had passed, although it was only two by Lynx's count. It wouldn't seem that this would be such torture, but it was. Every molecule in his body screamed to move. At one point, his nose began to itch, which added another exquisite layer to his pain. This was compounded by the knowledge that he not only had brought this on himself, but he had aided Skinner in taking Tesla to be abducted by some mysterious outside force.

*Who is Axios anyways?* he thought. Because of course, in the hours after Skinner's flight, what Lynx had was time to think. Time to go over every nuance of the conversation and time to think about Tesla. Did he hate her? Love her? She'd been betrayed by her own father, or primary producer, but she was also an A-One, and thus guilty of crimes of unbelievable inhumanity against his people. It was hard for Lynx to conceive of families that could do that to one another, but here it was. And, really, if A-Ones had no problem cloning themselves for cosmetic perfection, selling out family members wasn't such a stretch.

Lynx understood that Skinner was on his own special trip, thinking that Axios represented a race of supreme beings who had come to take the A-Ones to some transcendent place due to his brilliant programming. As young as he was, Lynx knew better.

What burned him more than the searing sensation of his

muscles screaming to move was what it meant to be a race of clones for A-Ones, or as he and his buddies commonly referred to them, vultures. *Turns out we picked the right nickname.* What hurt the most was what this meant for Phlox. He wanted to cry and scream but he couldn't, and so he had to sit with it.

*How could I be so stupid!* He tried to shake his head and failed. The cryogenic ray still glowed like an afterthought all over his skin. It didn't seem to be lessening. Lynx was acutely aware of the movement of air in and out of his lungs and the thudding woosh of his bloodstream. The only way he could gauge the time was by watching the next storm eclipse the setting sun. The weather was fiercely dramatic at this high vantage point. In stark contrast to his absolute immobility, the view outside the bank of windows and beyond the landing pad was a swirling maelstrom of wind and sand and whipping clouds over a smokily setting sun.

*How are they flying in this?*

After a long while, Lynx's mind wandered back to the time before. He didn't really want to think about those dark memories, but it was as impossible to steer his mind away from this shadowed place as it was to itch his nose. There wasn't much, he'd only been eight, but he did remember a woman with copper skin and dark hair, with a wide laughing mouth.

In this memory, she wasn't laughing, she was frantic. She was tucking a note into the blanket swaddling a bawling Phlox. It was hard for him to hear her hurried instructions over Phlox's wails. She kept glancing over her shoulder, which seemed odd to Lynx as they were the only ones in the pod. Her long wavy hair would whip him in the face every time she turned. And then she pushed him and his sister into the back storage closet, kissing him and telling him to remain very still and try to quiet his sister. He did pacify Phlox finally, rocking and singing her into a fitful sleep. He'd always had a knack for that. The last thing he remembered was falling asleep himself. Then everything went dark.

Back in Skinner's office, in an attempt to shake off his intrusive past, he tried with every fiber of his will to move, to break free of the ray's freezing power. Inside his clenched jaw he screamed, releasing the forced groan into the empty room. He pushed so hard with his mind he saw stars, and his vision began to eclipse into darkness, but he remained as frozen as ever.

An hour later, Lynx was considering how to alert the mech in the next room on its podium to help, although it was Skinner-programmed and would probably be useless and even more foolish than using a cryo-ray on a force-field. Suddenly he heard the door swoosh up behind him. He tried with all his might to turn and see who was there. He could hear the soft pad of steps toward him, could almost feel the presence of *some*one just behind him. He groaned/screamed again, there was no use in trying to hide. The stars exploded at the corners of his vision but still he pushed.

"Easy, boy-o," said a voice. "You're going to strain something."

Relief washed over Lynx and he went limp in the rigid cage of his body. Chick came into view, half-smiling although his eyes glinted with concern.

"You all right then?" he asked, pulling a makeshift tool out of his pocket, rotating the base on the object faster and faster until the lights along the side began to glow. "Hold on, we'll see if this will be enough to reverse the effects. Cryo-ray, am I right? Oh wait, you can't answer." From the base of the object, Chick pulled pulsing yellow pads the size of his thumb. He applied them to Lynx's temples, over his heart, and above both of his knees, as well as to his hand, the human one, which still gripped the metal one, pointing it toward the conference table. Chick took a look at Lynx's hand and followed the trajectory.

"Boy-o, really? You did this to yourself?" Chick guffawed, rotating the base of the tool even more quickly.

Lynx silently winced. The object in Chick's hands was glowing at a steady rate now. "Right, few more seconds and it should be at its highest resolution, and WHAM!" He pressed a button, the object in his hands jolting. Lynx felt as if the pads spurted red-hot wax, the burning trumping the pain of paralysis. The searing sensation spread in waves from every place on his body where Chick had applied the pads. When the burning reached his mouth, Lynx instinctually opened it to scream, his jaw cracking with relief. Soon the remedy had flooded all through his body and he collapsed at Chick's feet, panting. As the pain subsided, Lynx stretched, relishing the exquisite feeling of movement. Chick squatted down in front of him.

"How did you find me?" Lynx asked, when he could finally speak.

Chick peeled the pads off Lynx. "When I saw you were up here and you hadn't moved in awhile, I thought that you might need a hand. So I flew up here, toot sweet." He chuckled. "You mind telling me what in Dome you're doing here? Something in my gut tells me it has to do with that girl Wren told me about."

Lynx nodded, still furious. "We were going to show them that Botches have feelings, that we're intelligent, caring people who deserve to be treated as something better than they treat us. But Skinner, that's her primary producer, told us that Botches are their clones, used only if a stupid A-One needs a hand or something." Lynx looked at his metal arm, tears pricking his eyes. "Did you know? Have you known all along?"

"I know parts of it, and I had my suspicions. There was ... *information* passed from A-Ones to me, not a lot, but enough."

"Why didn't you say anything?"

Chick's voice became gruff. "I didn't know for sure, like I said, only parts. And the only way I knew how to deal with it was to fix it, to put on the prosthetics, to create weapons in the prosthetics, to keep Botches as whole as I could. Until I had proof."

"Now you have proof."

The two were silent for a while.

"How did this happen?" Chick gestured at the desk in front of them with the tool.

"They figured out who we were, I mean who I was, and that's when I blasted them. Or thought I blasted them. I really just blasted us, stupid protecto-field."

Chick gave a low whistle. "We'll definitely get you some practice with those new tools once we sort this all out. Do you remember what Skinner was talking about?"

Lynx told him what Skinner had said about Axios.

"Dome, that doesn't sound good." Chick stood and began to pace the long room. "Did the other programmer seem to agree with him?"

"No, Mendel thought Axios should be researched more."

"Mendel, huh? Now that's a familiar name." Chick stopped in front of Lynx, who was still sprawled out on the ground. "Maybe this will get the A-Ones off our backs? Although, since we're genetic copies of them, maybe not. Too risky." He started his pacing again. "I bet whatever they're doing, they're doing it at that complex I found."

"All right, let's go to the complex. Let's go help Tesla." Lynx creakily got to his feet.

"The only place we're going is home. Wren's worried sick."

"No way, Chick, seriously, I *owe* Tesla this much. I have to go after her. She saved me once, now it's my turn."

Chick considered this. "I appreciate that, bub, I really do, but these are A-Ones. They've been preying on us for decades. Why should we extend any help? I don't think so." He took Lynx's arm, tugging him toward the doorway. "No, Below is the only place we're going."

"Chick! I have to!" Lynx threw off his uncle's arm. "I love her."

Chick regarded him with the cool gaze of the older and wiser. "Fat lot of good it'll do you. Do you know why Wren became so furious when she figured out who Tesla was?"

"I thought it was to protect us."

"Undoubtedly, but there's more to it. She was once in love with an A-One, an Evolutionist. They were together for a long while, on the sly of course. And then one day, he left her, no explanation, nothing. And to top it all off, Slug's legs were taken soon afterward."

"Oh man," Lynx said.

"Don't think you're the first that's fallen for an A-One. It's a story that's as old as the Dome itself. It's an unbalanced relationship from the start. The ones who seem to get crushed are us, not them. That girl may say that she loves you and wants what's best for you, but she's an A-One. She always has been and always will be. Guard your own heart. She might take it as easily as she harvests a new part."

"Chick, whatever Axios is, it'd be a good idea to figure out its intentions, right? It's possible that it's a force for good, but if it's not, we need to be even more aware of its nature, don't you think?"

"It's true that if there's something else out there, we should know what it's up to. And it would give me a chance to explore that complex."

Lynx was as unmoving as if he was still under the effects of the cryo-ray, internally pleading as Chick debated with himself.

"All right, we'll go check it out."

Lynx whooped and leapt in the air.

"Checking it out does not mean getting ourselves into a sticky situation again, young blood. You will be under my command and you will not be throwing your cryo-ray around willy-nilly, you got me?"

Lynx quieted down. "Yes, yes sir. Absolutely. But we'll try and help Tesla out if we can, right?"

"If it happens that we can help the girl out at the same time as we are gathering information, then yes."

Lynx let out a second whoop.

"But that's a conditional," Chick admonished. "*If* we can help her out while we learn more, *then* we will. Only if."

"Got it."

Chick led an overly excited Lynx out of the room.

"Hey," Lynx looked at the back of the mech slumped over its podium. "How did you get by the robo-greeter?"

"Simple. I know where its off switch is." Chick held up the tool that had unfrozen his nephew and gave Lynx a wink. Sure enough, the mech was still and silent, forehead to the podium, eyes wide and dark.

Chick's boat was twice the size of Lilly's Par One and was sleek as a bullet. Its closed roof made it ideal for Chick's longer expeditions outside the Dome. It appeared to be shoddily made, but Lynx knew better. Botches had to slap together their machines from parts that the A-Ones cast off. The effect was that of a boat held together with twine and hope, but in reality, these were very sturdy vessels. Knowing Chick, there were probably other hidden extras. Lynx scaled the ladder after his uncle. When he reached the cockpit, he found Chick with his goggles on, sitting in the driver's seat, surrounded by touchpads of all shapes and sizes.

"Wow," Lynx said as he climbed in. "You've really tricked this one out."

"The Pteranodon? You bet," Chick said as he activated the many screens around him. He handed Lynx a pair of goggles and peered through the windshield in front of him. "Buckle in, boy-o," he barked at Lynx, "this may be a hot and heavy take-off. I hope I have enough energy …" He trailed off. Through the portholes on either side of him, Lynx could see two sails unfolding on the sides of the Pteranodon, their bio skins glowing orange.

"Chick? Aren't the sails supposed to be on the top of the boat?"

"Well yes, if you mainly stay on the land, which your Dimetrodon does, but the Pteranodon here, she doesn't stay on the ground." He turned a toothy grin on Lynx. Chick threw a final switch and the Pteranodon shuddered, settling into a rhythmic vibration. There was a slight lift and then Chick jammed a lever forward. The Pteranodon took off and began free falling toward the jagged ins-and-outs of Middlespace. Chick cranked a wheel to the left of the console and the boat roared to life, lifting them in a sudden swoop.

"How are we getting out?" Lynx asked him.

"There are ports up here as well, boy-o." Chick gestured at a point on the far side of the Dome, beyond the reaching branches of the A-Ones' domiciles. Against the darkness outside, the port showed up as a disc of lighter gray, encircled by yellow lights. "We have to type the code in remotely," continued Chick, flipping several levers at once, "as well as scramble the port's memory to make it 'forget' that we ever passed through. But that may be an unnecessary precaution."

"Why's that?"

Chick twisted in his seat to look his nephew fully in the face. "Because we may not be coming back."

There was no more conversation in the cockpit. As they neared the port, Lynx wondered if he really wanted it to open. Then, in slow motion, the doors of the circular port retracted and the Pteranodon passed through, to be immediately buffeted by the whipping winds outside. Chick struggled with the steering console. They had ejected themselves into a tornado twice the size of the Dome itself.

Debris whipped by the portholes, periodically slamming into the ship with shuddering force. Chick pushed the nose of the Pteranodon at a 45-degree angle toward the ground. Lynx held the sides of his seat in a death grip. The whole craft was shaking, and

Chick's jaw gritted hard as he tried to maintain a steady course. The tornado was pulling at the seams of the boat, close to rending the whole thing apart. A shrieking sound filled the cabin and a bright orange light began a hectic blinking on the console.

"She's not going to hold!" Lynx yelled at his uncle over the squawk of screaming metal.

"*Yes ... she ... is!*" Chick hollered, hands jerking left then right in an effort to hold true to his course. The high-pitched howl that came from both ship and wind reached an ear-splitting crescendo, and then ceased altogether. Lynx's skull pulsed with the sudden silence, which seemed even louder than the cacophony of a moment before. The violent thrashing of the boat had likewise stopped and Chick was having no trouble with the steering console as he continued gliding down.

"What?" Lynx looked out the window at the tornado's striated girth. A largish boulder whipped by them at an unheard-of speed. "How?"

"We're in the heart of the tornado, pretty quiet yeah?"

"Weirdly so. Nice going, Captain."

With a controlled thump, the Pteranodon alit on the ground and Chick activated switches. "Crank that. No, the one on your other side. Yeah, that should do it."

Lynx could feel the grip as the magnets took hold. Through the dirt-strewn windshield, the other wall of the tornado approached at a ferocious speed, bearing down on the piece of strapped-together metal that housed two very vulnerable people. It took hold of the ship like an iron fist, thumping down on the roof. Lynx could feel the fight between the howling winds and the powerful magnets. At one point, Lynx felt a puff of cold air on his neck, accompanied by a high whistling and the stink of ozone, and he realized that this could be the moment that the boat would be ripped apart. Yet immediately afterward, it settled back on its haunches as the tornado passed over them. The whistling lessened and then ceased altogether as the view outside the portholes cleared, revealing a stretch of inky sky, gray-brown jagged mountains, slick surfaces of the outer domes, and above that, a spattering of stars.

"That was a fierce one," Chick said, giving the console an affectionate pat. "But you are a peach, not going down yet, are you now?"

Lynx broke into a nervous giggle, which morphed into a full-scale giggling fit, soon joined in by Chick.

"What are we laughing about?" Lynx snuffled through guffaws.

"Who knows?" Chick replied when he was able. "But it's better than pissing ourselves." With that they rebounded into another full-scale fit, the sound of the the two men chortling filling the small cabin. When they tapered off, sides aching and cheeks sore, Chick disengaged the magnets, pushing the throttle forward, and the Pteranodon raced across the desert floor. Out the stern porthole, a plume of dirt kicked up in their wake as the boat carved through the landscape at an uncanny speed.

# CHAPTER SEVENTEEN

t was a few hours past the outer Rim before they reached their destination. The landscape was monotonous, stark desert strewn with rocks and debris from the countless scouring of storms, tornadoes, and the merciless scorching sunlight. The distant mountains remained static, seemingly never changing in dimension. When a shape suddenly appeared on the horizon, Lynx assumed it was another boulder. As they drew nearer, he could see that it had angles, and a few minutes later, pipes and shafts of large silos were visible. They sailed through metal gates made of discarded piping welded together and were surrounded by blocks of discarded metal, bins with bits and bobs all the way from large sheeting to tiny nuts.

*No wonder he got so worked up,* Lynx thought, glancing at his uncle's concentrated form hunched over the steering console. *This place is like Botch heaven.*

The rows and rows of metal storage stretched on for half a mile, and Chick's demeanor grew more tense with each passing second. When they passed the last of them, they entered what looked like an arena. Chick hung a sharp right, following a high metal wall made of hammered sheeting. A silo blossomed out of the base of the wall, the battered metal rising to a height of fifteen feet or so. A door hung ajar, revealing a dark passage behind it.

"This is where we get off," Chick said, ratcheting back the throttle and dimming the lights. The cockpit's roof popped off and the cabin filled with chilly night air tempered with a metallic tang. Lynx stood and stretched, his joints cracking. As they gathered what little gear they had and exited the Pteranodon, Chick explained that there was one part of the complex he'd not yet explored because he had heard noises there: humming and clanking.

"The double metal doors are really something. They're what really convinced me. Nobody puts doors that well made in front of a trash heap." Chick shook his head. "No, you put those doors in front of something you don't want someone getting to. Can you make that camo suit light our way?"

Lynx hadn't thought of that. To his cuff he said, "lights." Both of them had to shield their eyes from the suit's sudden transformation into a blinding block of incandescence. "Plain camo," Lynx said as quickly as possible, and just like that, the suit was a subtle swirl of brown and green. "Let's try that again. Glow," he said to his cuff. The suit began to glow a soft blue. "Brighter," he clarified and his body's emanations grew until it was a comfortable intensity.

"To be clear," Chick said. "You're going to save the girl if possible. I'm here for information."

Lynx nodded with resignation. They entered through the ominous rectangle and found themselves on the grated landing of a metal staircase that led down into the bowels of the earth. Chick led, Lynx followed, his suit illuminating their path from behind.

When they had gone down for a steady five minutes, the stairs ended on a bed of rough rock. A tunnel stretched ahead of them. The warm stagnant air trapped within smelled of creosote. The light from Lynx's suit washed over red rock walls with the ceiling only a few feet over their heads. They made their way along the trail, which zigged left and right in a nonsensical manner. As they walked, it grew narrower and narrower. Soon the walls were brushing either sides of Lynx's shoulders and he had to turn himself sideways in order to fit through the cramped passageway.

"Chick," Lynx said, anxiety evident in his voice. "Getting awful tight in here. What's up there?"

"Few more yards. It'll be a tight squeeze toward the end but we'll make it. What's the matter? Touch of claustrophobia?"

"Actually, yes," Lynx muttered.

It was a squeaker; they could barely shove through a slit of rock into the next chamber. When Lynx wrenched his body through the tiny opening and stepped into the next room, he found metal under his feet.

"We've arrived," Chick said, gesturing toward the far wall, which appeared to be made of many layers of different metals. Bands as thick as Lynx's arm bracketed the portal and there was a control touchpad to the right of the door, looking like an unblinking black eye. There was only one other place Lynx had ever seen such a formidable-looking doorway: Skinner's lab. Chick had his tool out, charging it up. He connected it to the control panel with a sensor pad and began typing frantically at it.

"You have to race the machine, in a virtual sense. It is trying to test you to see if you are another electrical current or a human being. Code, it allows; humans, it does not. I have to convince it that I am not a human and only then will it bypass the security system." Lynx was amazed Chick could talk and type at such speed. "Almost, almost …" Chick ceased to type, letting his hand fall to his side. He studied the door in front of him, a confused look crossing his features. With a beleaguered *swoosh* sound, the doors parted. Chick and Lynx flattened against the walls. Chick inched forward until he could peek around the corner. He straightened up and motioned for Lynx to follow him as he entered the room.

It was an antechamber of sorts, lit from an unseen source down a passage and around a corner, where they could hear people arguing. Chick and Lynx moved down the hallway and followed the voices as they grew louder. Lynx could recognize Skinner's voice from here, and Mendel's accented English, but he couldn't hear Tesla. Nerves started to tingle his skin as if he were being mildly electrocuted. *Or is it something else?* Lynx thought. Chick stopped him as they were making their final approach.

"Camo up, buddy, invisible-style. You're following my lead."

Lynx nodded, unquestioning. He set his suit on "match background" and pulled up the hood.

"This is for all the marbles." Chick was looking a little to the right of Lynx, holding up his fist. Lynx gave it a pound.

The voices became clearer as they went down the hall.

"You *can't*, you just *can't* without the proper research, man, it's just not done. You don't even know who or what we're dealing with," Mendel was saying, his voice cracking with passion.

Lynx and Chick rounded a final corner into a cavernous room with only a limited portion in the middle lit by banks of fluorescent lighting. From across the darkened floor, forty feet away, Lynx could make out Tesla's floating form. She was still glowing purple, with her hands outstretched in protest. Mendel was red with anger, shaking a fist in Skinner's face as the programmer worked at a bank of humming machines.

"I can and I will, Mendel." Skinner looked up at Tesla. "She is my product after all. I can do with her what I want."

"You don't know what they are, or what they want with her!" Mendel exclaimed. "Your own daughter!"

Chick was incautiously striding toward the tense group. All of sudden, a crackling sound rippled across the room, followed by roaring as undulating lights burst into life atop two poles, an electrical current stretching between their apexes and meeting in the middle.

*Right above Tesla,* Lynx noted with dread.

Skinner spoke above the rising, gyrating roar. "It's her destiny, fool. This is what it has been about all along. This is what she was made for. She is the most perfect of us and so *she* will lead us into our future." The roar thrummed at a higher rapidity, settling into a throbbing that soon took on the characteristics of a human voice.

"KG727," it boomed.

Skinner spun and spread his hands out. Lynx and Chick had stopped fifteen feet outside the circle of light.

"Have you brought X3721?"

"Yes, Axios, I have brought the product." He gestured toward the frozen form of Tesla. The light from the two towers met in a shower of sparks above her head, the raw current dripping over her like hot wax, running over her features until she was covered from head to toe with glowing, pulsing electricity that resembled incandescent maggots burrowing into her skin.

"Who is the other?" The voice's gender was hard to discern. It sounded as if there were three different voices woven together. Lynx shuddered.

"Another programmer." Skinner's posture was that of a supplicant before his idol.

Mendel took a step toward the arc of blinding light. "Axios, I am FZ367."

"Yes," Axios responded, the two pulsing lights throbbing with the voice's inflection. "I am aware of your production code. Impressive work you did, before they mind-wiped you. Pity, you were a very promising specimen."

"Again with the mind wipe!" Mendel sputtered.

Axios continued. "You were the one who made all this possible." A shower of sparks dripped off of Tesla's toes. "You were the one who perfected your genetic strands … for us."

Skinner looked startled, his forehead creased and his mouth opened. He took a cautious step forward. "For you?"

"You start to understand. Yes, for us. It's begun, thanks to you and your perfect product. With her genes we will be able to withstand the Asthenia. Splicing hers into our own genetic strands will enable us to clear our way for much progress."

Skinner shot a horrified glance at Mendel, who was as frozen as Tesla, stunned. "You can't be serious! Stripping her strands? That would mean that she would ... she wouldn't ... she'd cease to exist!"

"This is why we seeded your Dome in the first place, so that the specimens wouldn't be contaminated by other populations and would remain pure. Let us begin." The arc over Tesla pulsed and stretched into a broad band of crackling power, lowering toward the crown of her head.

Chick came to life. "Come on," he gestured to the general vicinity around him, having no idea where Lynx actually was. He strode, Lynx on his heels, into the circle of light. The shocked programmers turned toward Chick but made no move to restrain him. The air in the lit area smelled of burnt ozone and the sharp acrid sweat of fear. The pulsing towers of light dimmed a fraction. "Who is this?" the alien voice asked.

"Greetings and salutations from the Underdwellers, or, as we like to call ourselves, the Botches." Chick nodded his head toward Tesla's rotating form. Lynx, taking the hint, moved around the pair of programmers to take a spot below the left tower. Chick grinned, hands on hips. "Getting a taste of your own medicine I see. How do you like it, A-Ones, being a bunch of spare parts for unseen forces? Nasty feeling, don't you think?"

"This is hardly the same thing," sputtered Skinner.

Chick turned his burning gaze on him. "Really?"

"Who is this intruder?" Axios' voice rose until it trembled the very air around them.

Skinner stepped forward. "He is an Underdweller. He is one of the race of people Mendel and I created to provide a resource for A-Ones to maintain their genetic perfection."

"Then this 'Underdweller' has a point, does he not? Enough! There is work to be done!"

Arcs of purple light spilled from the tops of the towers, just missing Lynx as each one leapt and encased the two programmers and one Botch with webs of cryo-ray. The pulsing blob around Tesla brightened as her spinning form became a golden nimbus above Lynx. The thrum in the air increased and high above it was a muffled scream. As the blob stretched, it became translucent, and Tesla's body was pulled like electric taffy. Suddenly, her head snapped back and a swirling mist in the shape of a double helix was teased from her tense tendons.

*Time to be the hero.* Lynx twisted a dial on his wrist and his hand launched out, the silver wires stretching taut. His hand blasted into the bands of light and held, the current coursing through the wires and into Lynx's arm. The thrumming moved into the center of his brain as electricity flooded his body, and yet still he held on.

His skin felt as if it were being stripped off with a red-hot razor. He screamed and bright current jumped from his mouth. All he could see was a burning whiteness, but still Lynx held on. His vision eclipsed, black stars shooting in from his periphery; he felt as if the wires in his left hand were actually fraying from the effort to hold on to the hot madness. Above his own yelling, and Tesla's muffled shrieks, he heard the triple voice of Axios thundering, "What is that, what is happening?! KG727, answer me!"

All of a sudden, there was a series of popping sounds, each louder than the last. With a final boom and an impressive shower of sparks, the whole room fell into pitch darkness. Lynx collapsed, hand clanging uselessly as his body crumpled to the corrugated iron floor. The programmers and Chick all fell to their knees, freed from the cryo-ray. Tesla's form ceased glowing and dropped like a dead bird, unmoving.

# CHAPTER EIGHTEEN

The lights came on incrementally, it seemed to Tesla, but then again, she was just waking up. When she opened her eyes, the programmers were shakily getting to their feet. She watched Lynx retract his hand. It jerkily snaked across the floor with a rasping sound and reattached itself to his wrist-port.

A bank of fluorescent lights came up on the left side of the lab. The noise that accompanied Axios' voice started up with a burp, and then shut down again. Tesla's body felt like a thousand tons of scrap metal. Lynx was pulling himself across the floor toward her as she tried to move. She lay on her back, head awkwardly thrust to one side, like a petal crushed under a boot heel.

Sparks sputtered from the top of one tower, once and then twice, and the burning ball incandesced again, the vibration picking up power as more lights went on. By the time Lynx had reached Tesla's side and had pulled her into his arms, all the lights were up and the thrumming had reached maximum volume again. She felt as if she had no control over her body. Her head lolled back and her eyes stared up at the arcing currents.

"Tesla," Lynx said. He planted a soft kiss on her lips.

She finally focused on Lynx's face. "Lynx?"

Before he could answer, Axios' voice boomed through the

room. "Fools! KG727, bring your secondary product for genetic stripping NOW."

Skinner stood before the blinding bands of light humming with noise. "No," he said. "No, I will not."

The vibrating lessened. "What did you say?" Axios' voice was soft but menacing.

Skinner took another step forward. "I said no, I won't. This is a sham. I thought we were going to be partners. I cannot let you destroy the thing I love most in the world. You can have me, but you can't have my daughter."

"But you are not the strain we want," Axios countered.

"You can't have her!" he shouted, his face dappled with sparks. "Take me!"

"Daddy?" Tesla said, grabbing the fabric of his pant leg in confusion. Skinner glanced down at her with tenderness and caught her hand, giving her a sad smile. "It'll be all right, Tes. This is the only way. I can't have it any other way, knowing what I do now." A finger of light wrapped Skinner's body as he was lifted into the air, his hand jerking out of Tesla's.

"Daddy, no!" Tesla struggled to her feet. Skinner was covered in pulsing light, the electrified maggots swarming over his face, which was gazing sorrowfully at her. "NO!" she screamed in horror as she limped toward the scorching, screaming blob that was her father, shoving her hand into the midst of the glowing goop as the lights all burst into brilliance. The mist twirled into double helixes above Skinner's head as his body was stretched beyond perception; the sound made Tesla's mind ache.

The light became blinding as Tesla's shrieks mixed with Skinner's. Green helixes glowed brighter than the incandescent blob and then *pop!* Skinner was gone and Tesla was once again crumpled on the floor. She looked up at where Skinner had been, but there was nothing except an afterglow outlining the shape of his body. In her shock she couldn't understand what had happened. Her mind kept seeing his form hanging above her and then she'd blink, only to have him disappear again.

"Skinner," Tesla whispered, silver tears gilding her ashen cheeks. The last hours had been the worst of her life. As much as she had bristled under Skinner's stiff control of her, and as much as she detested him for what she'd learned that afternoon, she also loved and admired him. And now he was gone. Gone for good. Try as she might, she couldn't shake the last image of him looking at her as the electricity swarmed over his features. Lynx folded her into a hug as she sobbed.

"He did the right thing," Chick said gruffly, walking around a stunned Mendel to where Tesla clutched Lynx. "There now, lass, it'll be all right. That's the way it's supposed to work. He goes first. Let's have a look at that hand."

Tesla lifted her arm in front of her face; where her right hand should have been the skin was smooth. It was as if there had never been a hand there at all. Her eyebrows twisted for a moment in horror and confusion. *Oh Dome, my hand … my hand is gone!* Tesla opened her mouth but couldn't make a sound.

"It's all right, you can install a new one," Lynx said. The look on his face told Tesla how much it hurt him to suggest that. Mendel shuffled his feet. A latent shower of sparks popped off, raining down on her like a bioluminescent waterfall.

Tesla gazed at Lynx. "No," she said. "That ends now. We have a new enemy to contend with." Conviction rang through her voice like a bell. She slipped her only hand into Lynx's human one as she turned to Chick. "Make me a Botch."

# APPENDIX

**Darwin**: Charles Darwin (1809-1882) English naturalist who posited that all species derive from a single species. Also championed the theory of evolution as well as natural selection, in which the struggle for existence creates selective breeding.

**Tesla:** Nikola Tesla (1856-1943) Serbian-born scientist, engineer, inventor and futurist. He is best known for his contributions in developing the alternating current electrical supply system. He came to the U.S. to work under Thomas Edison and soon struck out on his own to continue exploring high-power and high-voltage experiments.

**Pav(lov):** Ivan Pavlov (1849-1936) Russian physiologist who made many important discoveries, especially the concept of conditioned reflex, which he developed after studying the amount and rate of salivation in dogs. In the experiment, a bell would ring whenever food was presented to dogs. The dogs would salivate when presented with the food. Eventually, they would salivate when they heard the bell, associating it with food.

**Schrodinger:** Erwin Schrödinger (1887-1961) Austrian physicist who contributed mostly to the field of quantum physics. Schrödinger's cat is a thought experiment in which a cat could be both dead and alive at the same time, per a random prior event.

**Kinsey:** Alfred Kinsey (1894-1956) American biologist, a professor of zoology and entomology, and sexologist. His studies of human sexualtiy provoked controversy in the 1940's and 1950's.

**Skinner:** B.F. Skinner (1904-1990) American psychologist, behaviorist, writer, inventor, and social philosopher. He created the Skinner box, or the operant conditioning chamber, which is a laboratory device used to study behavior and conditioning in experiments. He believed that free will was a farce and that any human action was the result of consequences. If an action produced negative consequences, he theorized, it would not be repeated. If it had positive ones, it often would. He called this reinforcement.

**Lilly:** William Lilly (1602-1681) English astrologist. Born to a yeoman in Leicestershire, Lilly went to London as a youth to take up a servant's position. Seven years later, he secured his fortune by marrying his master's widow, which allowed him to write about astrology. He published *Christian Astrology* in 1647, the first compendium about astrology to be published in English rather than in Latin. He was a controversial character and was both aided and abused by his powerful associates.

**Carver:** George Washington Carver (1864-1943). American scientist, botanist, educator and inventor. He was born into slavery in Missouri. His research into and promotion of crop rotation suggested alternating such crops as soybeans, peanuts, and sweet potatoes with the cotton that was usually grown in that area, which depleted the nutrients in the soil. Rotation would help reintroduce key nutrients back into the soil as well as providing food for farm families. His most popular practical bulletin (of which he published 44) described 105 recipes using peanuts.

**Mendel:** Gregor Mendel (1822-1844) Polish scientist and Augustinian friar. He gained fame after his death for being the "father of modern genetics." His work demonstrated that certain traits in pea plants follow particular patterns, which became known as Mendel's Laws of Inheritance. His work was lauded only after the turn of the 20th century.

**Sagan:** Carl Sagan (1934-1996) American astronomer, astrophysicist, cosmologist and author. He was a professor at

Cornell, published more than 200 scientific papers and was the author, co-author, or editor for more than 20 books. He firmly advocated the Search for Extraterrestrial Intelligence or SETI.

**Avicenna:** (980-1037) Persian polymath. He wrote 450 treatises on a variety of subjects. His most famous works were *The Book of Healing* and *The Canon of Medicine.*

**Locke:** John Locke (1632-1704) English philosopher and physician. He is widely known as the Father of Classical Liberalism. His theory of mind postulated that the human mind was a blank slate or *tabula rasa* and that our knowledge is all derived from experience.

**Dimetrodon:** Early Permian dinosaur whose most distinguishing feature was the large sail on its back formed by spines on its vertebrae. It was probably one of the top predators of the Permian period. Its sail may have been used to heat or cool its body by thermoregulation.

**Pteranodon:** A large flying reptile of the late Cretaceous period. A male's wingspan could stretch up to 18 feet; a female's 12 feet.

**Parvicursor:** The name means "small runner" and it was one of the smallest and fastest dinosaurs in the late Cretaceous period.

**Calliope:** The Greek muse of epic poetry.

**Thalia:** The Greek muse of comedy.

**Clio:** The Greek muse of history.

**Pandora:** In classic Greek mythology, Pandora was the first human woman created by Hephaestus and Athena on the instructions of Zeus. Her myth tells us that, out of sheer curiosity, Pandora opened a box, unleashing all the evils of the world, leaving only Hope inside.

**Sylph:** Mythological creature of the western tradition. According to Paracelsus, sylphs were invisible beings that were elementals of the air.

**Asthenia:** In Greek, lack of strength or weakness.

**Axios:** From the Greek, being in balance.